RHYTHM OF THE KNIFE

MEREDETH CONNELLY MIND HUNT THRILLERS
BOOK 5

E.H. Vick

DARK TRIAD PUBLISHING

NEW YORK

Dark Triad Publishing
769 Broadway #1060
Manhattan, NY 10003

Publisher's Note: This is a work of fiction. Names, characters, places, and incidents are a product of the author's imagination. Locales and public names are sometimes used for atmospheric purposes. Any resemblance to actual people, living or dead, or to businesses, companies, events, institutions, or locales is completely coincidental.

Rhythm of the Knife/ E.H. Vick. -- 1st ED.
ISBN 978-1-951509-23-1

TABLE OF CONTENTS

DEDICATION

In memory of my uncle, Porter Van Zandt, and for my aunt, Debra Mooney Van Zandt, and my cousin, Kirstin Mooney, who lived in Sherman Oaks.

I hope you enjoy *Rhythm of the Knife*. If so, please consider joining my online community—details can be found at the end of the last chapter.

CHAPTER 1
AUTUMN OF TERROR
Los Angeles, CA

MICHAEL DRUITT WATCHED the pretty little brunette assess the darkened alley. She stood in the sickly cone of light shining down from a streetlight badly in need of maintenance. It was late—or early, depending on your point of view—somewhere after three in the morning, but not yet four, and she appeared exhausted. Druitt knew she'd just finished a shift and a half at the hospital three blocks away, and he knew the brunette's name: Mary Ann Blocker.

She glanced at the empty street behind her, then turned her attention to the street in front of her before shifting her gaze back to the dark alley. Druitt had made sure it was dark—a silenced pistol had taken care of the lights hung by both the city and the property owners, and shattered glass lay about like so much confetti.

He loved Blocker's tight little body, and he loved the way her yellow scrubs accented her curves. He suspected she bought one size small to emphasize her womanly wiles. *She's a slut*, he thought. *She deserves this*. He had a long history of hating easy women that stemmed back to an incident in his late teens—an incident in which he'd felt used and abused. *Come on, Mary Ann! There's no one hiding in this alley...except me, that is.*

She turned to face the alley and drew a deep breath, steeling herself to take her accustomed shortcut to the parking garage two blocks over. It was clear she didn't like the darkness, but he'd also taken measures to ensure the street was dark as well. He'd left the streetlight under which she stood and several others chosen at random. She'd think it was a problem with the power grid—at least that's what he hoped.

Blowing her breath out through pursed lips in an almost whistle, Mary Ann stepped out of the penumbra of weak light and, clutching her bag under her arm, she stepped into the mouth of the alley. Michael took a slow breath, ensuring he made very little, if any, sound. He held his left hand behind his back, and in it, he clutched the long-bladed Liston knife. He'd spent hours polishing and sharpening the knife, then had sterilized it in an autoclave. He had other instruments with him as well, but they were for later. He focused his thoughts, visualizing the first cut, the left-to-right slash across poor Mary Ann's throat. He would lunge out of the shadows from her right, the eight-inch blade already arcing toward her throat. She would have no time to defend herself, no time to evade the blow. He stilled himself, barely breathing, and forced himself to wait for the perfect moment.

Anticipation built and built as Mary Ann advanced slowly into the alley. *Good God, hurry up!* he thought at her. Her knuckles had gone white on the canvas strap of her bag, which bulged under her arm. He had no doubt her palms were sweating, no doubt her vision and brain worked in concert to paint a rapist in every shadow, behind every dumpster and trash can, and Druitt imagined he could hear her pulse thundering from her carotid.

She drew near, and his grip tightened on the Liston, the muscles of his left arm engorging with blood. He forced himself to stand still, forced his feet not to shuffle, and she drew nearer still. Her eyes were wide, dilated to take in as much light as possible, but she didn't see him. Perhaps she sensed him, but in modern society, few gave credence to the irrational shouts in the back of their minds.

That's what made his chosen profession so much easier.

She stepped within range, but it would still be a reach, so Michael remained frozen in place—a black shadow amidst other black shadows. She scanned the alley from her left to her right, her gaze skipping right past him. She took another step, then halted. "Wuh…" She cleared her throat and tried again. "Who's there?"

Druitt grinned but, of course, said nothing.

She peered around the alley again, then shrugged and took another step.

Druitt lunged out of the shadows made by the bump out of the apartments on the second floor and the shrub hiding the pillar between two roll-up doors, the Liston's blade a silver arc that would bisect her throat with ease. Her gaze darted to him, her gaze found his, and for a moment, he saw recognition there.

But then the knife had completed its arc, and he'd barely felt the impact. Mary Ann's blood jetted into the air, and being a registered nurse, she did the right thing: she tucked her chin and grasped her throat with both hands, staggering back. Her bag fell to the crumbling macadam with a *thump* and the sound of glass breaking.

Michael took another rapid step forward, closing the distance between them. With his right hand, he grabbed her by the hair and jerked her head back and up, peering into her eyes. He saw her plan a moment before she tried it, but a moment was all he needed, and her knee glanced off his thigh instead of slamming into his groin. She didn't dare use her hands or risk passing out in moments—one of the reasons he enjoyed the throat slash as his opening move—but she tried with the other knee, nonetheless. He countered that blow as well, his grin stretching and stretching.

Her mouth worked, but she couldn't make a sound thanks to the deep bite of the Liston knife. He'd severed her trachea and esophagus as well as her carotids and jugulars. The blackness spilling from between her fingers was a mix of arterial and veinous blood, and she had only seconds of consciousness remaining, a few seconds more of life.

She tried again with her knee, but the blow was weak and ineffectual against his thigh. She floundered backward, trying to create space between them, and he let her go.

"Mary Ann, stop all this foolishness," he said and saw the confirmation of her suspicions in her eyes. "Yes, you know me, and I know you." He pulled the balaclava off his head and grinned at her, enjoying the relatively cool air across his cheeks. "Come, we both know you are already dead."

She turned and stumbled toward the mouth of the alley, reeling like a drunk, stumbling over her own two feet. He chuckled as she tried to run, then listed to the left and fell into the ground cover lining the right side of the alley.

"See there?" he asked. "I'd say you have seconds, Mary Ann, so let me assuage your curiosity. I chose you because you're a slut, a dirty little whore. Your tight uniforms, your bouncing little ass. You *are* beautiful, especially your eyes. I don't think I've ever seen a hazel so bright. But...unfortunately, I can't abide a woman of low morals, a seductress, a slut."

She rolled to her back and looked up at him, her eyes imploring him to help. She didn't dare shake her head, not with the death grip she maintained on her throat, not if she valued her last few moments as a living woman, but he could see the denial in her eyes, and it enraged him.

"Don't pretend I'm wrong!" He strode to her, bent, and pulled her hands from her throat. She had no strength left to fight him—even the arterial jetting from her severed arteries had weakened to a gush.

She thrashed from side to side, her mouth forming words she didn't have the air to speak. She tried to kick him, but it was no more effective than the knees to the groin had been.

"You're a dirty little whore, Mary Ann, and I'm going to make sure the world knows. They will call me 'Jack,' which is quite a compliment, really." He cocked his head to the side. "Do you believe in a god or gods, Mary Ann?" Her eyes were glazing, rolling from side to side, and her struggles had weakened to the point that he hardly needed to counter them. "Do you? A simple nod will suffice." She blinked rapidly, trying to focus her eyes, looking past him, looking through him. "Who do you see? Mary Ann? *What* do you see?" A momentary regret flashed through him. She'd never make another sound, which meant he'd never get an answer.

Her eyes rolled, and her mouth made gasping, fish-like movements. The gush from her neck became a sluggish dribble, then stopped altogether. He felt the rush, reveled in it, throwing his head back and releasing a satisfied sigh. Then he dropped her wrists, watching her arms flop to her sides. He stared down at her a moment, then turned and jogged back to his gear, retrieving the other surgical instruments he'd brought with him and arraying them beside Mary Ann Blocker's cooling corpse.

He knelt astride her legs, his butt resting on her knees, and reached for one of his custom knives, the one he'd fitted with a number ten scalpel blade, and started cutting.

CHAPTER 2

JACK'S BACK

Quantico, VA

JIM MCCUTCHINS CALLED Meredeth as she strolled down the hall with Michelina—or Dana Jensen as the FBI knew her. They'd discussed Lucy in great detail, and it was clear the diminutive woman would be a dead end as far as interviewing her went.

Meredeth stopped walking. "One second, Dana. I've got to get this."

Michelina nodded and pulled out her own phone, staring intently at the screen.

"What's up, boss?" asked Meredeth after accepting the call.

"My office. I have a formal request for your services."

"Where to this time?"

"California, again."

Meredeth thought she heard a hesitation, a bit of heartbreak, in Jim's voice as he named the state.

"But Southern California, this time. Los Angeles."

"Ah. The City of Angels and all its assorted demons."

"Yes. My office, now."

"Right, chief. I'll just collar Van Zandt and—"

"No need. He's on his way."

"Oh, okay. Then so am I."

McCutchins hung up without another word, and Meredeth smiled at Michelina, then shook her head. "Sorry, Dana. We've got to cut this short."

"Catch a case?"

Meredeth nodded. "Los Angeles."

Michelina frowned. "I suspected there was someone out there. You know, warming up."

"Oh?"

"Yeah. There's been a few disappearances in the homeless community—all women."

"Disappearances, but not murders?"

"Of course, I believe they were murdered, but there are no bodies, and the homeless population is transient by nature. The women could have simply moved on."

"But you don't think so?"

"No."

"Care to share why you feel that way?"

Michelina shook her head. "I can't say, not really. It's just a feeling I get when I look at data models sometimes."

"Uh-huh. What about the data—"

"I really don't know, Meredeth. It could be something with the timing of the disappearances or the similarity between their living arrangements. It could be nothing. I could be totally wrong."

"I don't know, Dana. I tend to think of you as an expert at seeing unknown crimes in the data sea you play in."

"Thanks for the vote of confidence, but I'm wrong as often as I'm right."

"Or are always right and we just don't know enough about the cases where we can't find anything."

"Maybe. Go on, though, Meredeth. Go talk to McCutchins, but I'd like to be kept in the loop on this."

"Sure. I'll call once we know something. Maybe it will shake the trees a little bit, and you'll find what you need to on those disappearances." Michelina nodded, then turned away and walked in the direction of the data analysis section. Meredeth went the other direction, back toward the BAU offices and, more specifically, Jim's office.

It took only a few moments to get there, and as she stepped into the office, she nodded to Jim, then sat beside Bobby. "What's going on in L.A.?" she asked.

"A body in an alley," said Jim.

"Just once, I'd like a serial killer to leave a body somewhere nice, somewhere that doesn't smell like garbage and excrement."

"Noted, but I doubt we'll find anything like that."

"There's always hope, Jim. Tell me about the bodies."

"Well, right now, there's only one."

She frowned, bunching her eyebrows. "One? Then it can't be classified as a serial murder."

"I know that, Connelly," said Jim, "but if you'll let me continue, you'll understand why I'm granting the LASD's request for profiler assistance."

"Sorry." She lifted her hands to shoulder level, palms toward Jim.

"Right. The victim was Mary Ann Blocker, a nurse at Kindred Haven Hospital in Sherman Oaks. She was found in an alley three blocks from the hospital—roughly between the hospital and the parking lot reserved for hospital staff. The local detectives say the alley is a shortcut that reduces the walking distance by four blocks."

"Robbery?" asked Bobby.

"No. Her wallet was in her bag, along with some jewelry, and her watch wasn't taken. Her throat was cut from left to right from the victim's perspective. The ME says she clamped both hands on the wound, but that only delayed the inevitable. The wound was just too deep, and it severed her trachea and esophagus. Even if she'd clamped the arteries and veins in her neck with enough force, she'd have drowned from the blood pouring into her lungs from internal injuries in her throat."

"Left to right? So, facing her, right to left. A right-handed killer would leave a cut going the opposite direction from his perspective. A southpaw," said Meredeth.

"Or someone smart enough to pretend he's left-handed to throw us off the track," said Bobby.

"The ME says no. The wound was deepest on the right, and the blood splatter thins out to the left. Left-handed or not, the killer struck with his left hand and with enough force to cut deeply and make it through the anterior portion of her throat in a single blow. The ME says he nicked a vertebra and would certainly have severed the cord otherwise. Based on the blood at the scene, she fought him, then tried to run, but as I said earlier, it wouldn't have mattered if she'd eluded him."

"A single laceration? No other wounds?" asked Meredeth.

"Oh, no. The cut to her throat was inflicted antemortem, but the rest came postmortem. He cut her abdomen from the bottom of the ribs along the right side to the bottom of her pelvis. Another, ragged wound appeared left of her stomach and was deep enough to cut the omentum. He inflicted two stabbing wounds in her genitalia, and three inches from her left side in the lower abdomen he gave her another jagged cut that ran very deep. On the right side at the same level, he cut her four times, parallel wounds of moderate depth."

"Oh, is that all?" Bobby smiled as he said it.

"Nope," said Jim. "He also inflicted postmortem bruises to her—"

"Let me guess," said Meredeth with a sour expression on her face. "A bruise here"—she pointed to her lower right jaw—"another here"—she raised her finger to her left cheek—"as if he grabbed her by the mouth using a forefinger and thumb. Did she also have one an inch below her jaw on the left side?"

Jim frowned at her. "Yes. And you're correct about the first two. How did you—"

"And her name was Mary Ann?"

Jim nodded, then made a pulling gesture with his hand.

"Mary Ann Nichols, boss."

"No, her last name was Blocker."

Meredeth shook her head. "Think Whitechapel. Mary Ann Nichols was Jack the Ripper's first confirmed victim. Her wounds—"

"I thought that was Mildred Tabram?" asked Bobby.

"No, her wounds were inconsistent with the rest of the series. Two knives were used—one a thick, heavy blade, and the other a dagger. Blocker's wounds are duplicates of those inflicted on Nichols."

"Oh, *Christ*," muttered Jim. "A Ripper copycat?"

Meredeth shrugged. "Looks that way. I see why they requested help with only one body. Was she found on August 31?"

Jim ruffled through his notes. "Yes. A garbage crew trying to get the dumpsters in the alley reported the crime at half past five that morning."

"Well, if he sticks to the pattern, that gives us seven days until the next one."

"And four more victims?" asked Jim.

"Four more verified, yes. If he goes by the letters, there may be six more."

Jim sighed and shook his head. His emotions were close: anger, grief, hate, but Meredeth knew those were directed at Kahin Alshaytan and Anya Seneca, a.k.a. Lucy. "Go on," he grated. "Talk to Melanie. Get flights this morning if you can. If you can't, let me know and I'll arrange a jet. Stop this guy, Meredeth. Don't allow him to complete the series."

"We'll do our best, boss," said Meredeth. She stood and motioned for Bobby to follow her. They left the office and stopped by Melanie's desk to ask her to arrange their flights, rental car, and accommodations, then to pass it all on to the LA County Sheriff's Homicide Division. "Jim says if you can't get us flights this morning, to let him know, and he'll get us a jet."

"Check," said Melanie. "I assume you're going home to pack?"

"No need," said Meredeth. "We have go-bags here."

"Very good. I'll email the details to you both."

"Thanks, Melanie. You're the best."

"I am, aren't I?" she asked with a smile.

"Hey, do you have access to the academy rolls?"

"Yes. Shall I look him up?"

Meredeth blushed a little. "I only want to know if he's in class or on a break so I can tell him about the travel."

Melanie fought against a knowing smile, then dropped her gaze to her computer's monitor when she lost. "Let me see." She clacked away at her keyboard at about six million characters a second, then nodded. "Yep. He's on a free hour."

"Okay, thanks," said Meredeth. She turned and walked down the hall to their squad room, then to her desk. She looked around and grunted as Bobby sauntered in. The room was full of chatter, and she shook her head while leaving. The hall was better.

CHAPTER 3

HOLLYWOOD DREAMS

Quantico, VA

MEREDETH DIALED KEVIN'S private cell number and put her phone to her ear. He picked up on the second ring, but the background reverberated with the bangs and pops of the firing range.

"Just a second, Mere," said Kevin. "Let me get out of here."

"Sure." She waited, glancing around surreptitiously as if she were a teenager cutting class to sneak a call to her boyfriend. Other agents strolled down the hall toward the cafeteria or elsewhere in the building, and some waved to her, but no one spoke.

"Okay, is this better?"

The bangs and pops had turned into muted bangs and pops, but she could hear him much better and said so. "I thought you'd be on a break, though. I had Melanie check the schedule."

"We are on a break. I'm helping some of the younger students with their shooting. You'd be surprised how awful some of them are."

"No, I wouldn't." She chuckled. "Tell them the back plate trick."

"Back plate trick?"

"Yeah, you know. The back plate of the pistol is in line with the barrel, so put it over the place you want the bullet to go."

"Ah, that's interesting."

"Works very well with a Glock."

"I'll pass that on. Kind of halfway between iron sights and point-shooting."

"Exactly. An old friend who retired from SEAL Team Six taught that to me."

"And if anyone would know all the tricks..."

"That's right."

"FBI, I love talking to you, but I'm sure you didn't call in the middle of a workday to chat."

"No, I didn't."

"Where to this time?"

"Los Angeles County."

"Oh, Hollywood! I've always wanted to be one of those technical consultants."

"I'll see if I can arrange that."

"I take it we'll need to postpone the packing trip to Hanable's Valley?"

"Most likely."

"How many vics?"

"Just one so far, but it's pretty clear there will be more."

"What? He's not even earned his serial killer tag."

"I'm sure he has," she said, "and probably many times over. But the body we have...it's a copycat crime, and that series had between five and seven victims dropped on a specific time frame. He's gone to extreme lengths to match the previous set of murders—right down to making sure the victim had the same first name as the first of that older series."

"Hmm. I'm guessing the original crimes took place in Whitechapel?"

"Got it in one. You sure you want to waste your time with teaching and HRT?"

"Oh, boy, am I. I'll let you do the profiles, then I'll sweep in at the end and make the collars."

She smiled with one side of her mouth. "I hadn't thought of that."

"All joking aside, Mere, if we need to put off the trip, we can do that. I can still head up there and get the place cleaned up so I can list it. Maybe the buyer will want the furnishings."

Meredeth's smile slid downward, morphing into a frown. "I..."

"You, what, Mere?"

Shaking her head, she said, "Never mind. It's nothing."

"Meredeth Lynne, say what you're thinking. Didn't anyone ever teach you to observe, communicate, *then* take action?"

"A million years ago. It's really—"

"If you say, 'nothing,' I'm coming over there to give you a spanking."

She chuckled at that. "It's just that I was kind of hoping you'd hang on to your house."

"In case things here don't work out?"

"What? No, no. Things here *will* work out, Kevin Saunders. Do you hear me?"

"Yes, ma'am! But if not for that reason, then..."

"I was hoping we could use it as a vacation home. We could go up there on weekends and spend our days looking for secluded spots in the woods. We could go out in the evenings, or walk, or—"

"Or find secluded spots in my bedroom."

"Yes."

"I mean, *our* bedroom."

"Right."

"Hmm. I'll have to consider it."

"I know. Don't feel like you have to if finances dictate—"

"No, it's nothing like that, Mere. I was going to sell it so I didn't have to worry about maintaining it. And maybe I still should. We could buy a vacation property with the proceeds—somewhere that's actually a vacation destination."

"Hanable's Valley is such a sweet place, though, Kevin. And I'll always think of it as a 'destination.' Especially after spending so much time there and meeting so many of your neighbors."

"Let me look into it."

"Okay."

"Let's get back to Hollywood."

"Sherman Oaks."

"*Hollywood*, I said."

"Don't make me come out there and spank you, Saunders. It would embarrass you in front of all your new friends who can't shoot."

Kevin chuckled. "Yeah, not to mention the instructors I'll be working with as soon as I graduate."

"Right."

"When do you leave?"

"Melanie hasn't made the arrangements yet, but Jim wants us out there today."

"Let me guess—he wants you to figure it all out before another body hits the pavement."

"Bingo. It may not be possible. I won't know until I get to the scene and see what he left me."

"Be careful, FBI."

"I always am, FBI."

Kevin chuckled. "Yeah, maybe that nickname doesn't work so well anymore."

Her phone gave a soft chime. "I think Melanie sent over my itinerary. I'll forward a copy to you."

"And call me after hours tonight. We end at seven."

"Okay. Are you staying in the dorms?"

"I might as well if you're out of town."

"Don't pick up any hot young FBI trainees who can't shoot, because *I can*."

Laughter rolled across the line. "I know it, Mere, and let me just say that 'hot' and 'young' don't hold a candle to 'hot' and 'brilliant' and 'sexy' and 'Meredeth.'"

"You better believe it, Saunders," she said through a grin. "And ditto."

CHAPTER 4
TRUTH AND CONSEQUENCES
David Branch's Farm, NY

CARL NARROWED HIS eyes and shook his head slowly. Lucy stood before him, her fingers wrestling with one another, tears streaming down her cheeks, her eyes red-rimmed and wet, her lips trembling. "I *killed* Jonathon for you!" he snapped. "I carved out his heart, remember? I can't take that back, no matter how contrite you pretend to be."

"I... I'm *not* pretending, Carl. I...I...luh..." She shook her head and dashed the tears from her overflowing eyes. "I had to do *something*, Carl. He would have raped me, eventually. Or killed me. Are those eventualities you want?"

"You used me, Lucy. You lied to my face, you...you...*manipulated* me."

"I..." She hung her head and sobbed. "Carl, *please*..."

"How am I supposed to go back to trusting you?"

"But I couldn't face him myself, Carl! He was too big, too strong."

"How are you going to make your way in the world, Lucy? Do you plan on manipulating *everyone* around you, *all the time*?"

She lifted her head, a modicum of defiance in her teary eyes. "And why not? I'm good at it!"

"Yeah," he scoffed. "I guess you are. Stay away from me, Lucy."

"No, Carl! Don't say that! I'm *sorry!*" She broke into a string of wet sobs, dropping her head forward so her hair hung in front of her face. "I did what I did because I couldn't see another way. If I'd come to you—"

"Which is what you *should have done*, Lucy. I'd have helped you. I'd have taken that fat pig on just because he was threatening you."

"But you wouldn't have killed him. You'd have beaten him up, but all that would have accomplished would be to make him hate me more. This was the only thing I could think of."

"You don't know what I might have done. Neither do I. Unfortunately, we'll never find out. What else have you lied to me about?"

"Nothing, Carl. *Nothing!* And I didn't lie about being scared Jonathon would kill me. Just about the beating and the rape."

"Who beat you up? The truth this time."

"I..." She shook her head and dropped her gaze to the floor. "It was Alex."

"And why?"

She lifted her head, eyes blazing. "Does it matter? Alex beat me badly, and I saw an opportunity. I took it, *just like Father taught me.*"

Carl shook his head, then covered his face with his hands. "Do you know what you've done to me? I'll have to tell Alex. I'll have to—"

"Alex knows."

"—tell Father. Do you know what he'll do to me? *You* won't get in trouble—you're practicing your art...but me? You led me around by the nose, and Father won't like that at all."

"You don't have to tell him. Alex will keep quiet."

"And you know this? You know *him*?"

"I know him enough to know he will keep his word to me. He didn't like Jonathon any more than Father did. Or us for that matter."

Carl shook his head. "What's worse than showing weakness? I'll tell you: it's showing weakness and then trying to cover it up. That's how you get killed around here."

"Listen, Carl, Father will be glad Jonathon's dead. He was going to order Alex to do it soon. Everyone knows that."

"Oh? You know Father's mind, too?"

"You saw how he interacted with Jonathon...like he was sorry to have saved him."

"Let's get back to my question. What else did you lie to me about? And don't say, 'nothing.' You don't become an expert liar like you are by telling one lie."

Lucy dropped her gaze. "I'm sorry you no longer trust me, Carl. I'd hoped..."

"What? You'd hoped we'd stick together? That we'd get married, and I'd kill whoever you told me to? I'm destined for better, Lucy. I'm destined for greatness. I'm destined to eclipse you, to eclipse Alex, Mack. Maybe even Father, but I won't fulfill that destiny if Father kills me."

"And what's wrong with sticking together? We make a good team."

"Teammates don't have to lie to each other."

She collapsed to the edge of her bed, then sat there, shoulders slumped, head lowered, gazing at the carpet, and tears fell from her eyes, sluiced down her cheeks, then ran onto her chin, where they fell to the floor. "Carl...I'm... You're right. I should have trusted you to help. I shouldn't have manipulated you." She lifted her tear-streaked face and gazed into his eyes. "I'm so sorry. I wish I could go back, could do everything over. Can you forgive me? Can we work to get back to the relationship we had? The relationship I—"

"*Ruined!*" he snapped.

"Please, Carl," she said in a voice that shook and quavered, a voice that sounded like tears. "I'll make it up to you, I swear, and if Father ever finds out, I'll make him understand that I'm to blame, not you."

"You just don't get it, Lucy," Carl said and sighed, shaking his head. "Father wants us to be strong. Having you step in and try to save me will be another nail in my coffin."

"But—"

"No buts, Luce." He turned toward the door but stopped halfway. "Did... I mean, before this, did you really..."

"Like you? Yes, I genuinely did—do. You are the first guy I ever cared about, Carl, and you're just perfect. Everything that happened...my fault, all of it. I just hope you can forgive me in time."

"Yeah, maybe."

"I'll be here waiting, Carl. If you ever need anything, I'm your girl. And I mean anything. You need relief? Come to my room and I'll get you off. We can make it like it was, like in the beginning when we enjoyed each other's bodies without...without..." She stopped, watching Carl's back as he walked out and closed her door behind him.

She turned off the waterworks and sat up straight, wiping away the tears with a corner of her bedclothes. She thought it had gone well, thought Carl would be back. Maybe he would hold out until the next time he was horny, but he'd come back to her arms, and when he did, she'd start sowing the seeds for a longer, more permanent relationship.

The thought made her smile.

CHAPTER 5

TAKING THE TOUR

Los Angeles County, CA

THE BUREAU GULFSTREAM G650 settled on its shock absorbers as the Rolls Royce BR725 engines wound down like dying banshees, their shrieking reverberating in the confines of the metal-walled hangar and concrete floor. The flight had taken only a little more than three and a half hours—which was the benefit of a custom flight at just under the speed of sound.

Meredeth turned her attention from her window and unfastened her seatbelt. Bobby was already up, of course, having taken one step back as was his habit to allow her to go in front of him. He got her purse and laptop case out of storage, then placed them on his seat for her convenience. She shouldered both and stepped into the aisle.

The pilot stepped out of the cockpit and leaned against the forward bulkhead. "What's the case this time?"

Grinning at the man—the same pilot who'd flown them to Saint Petersburg—Meredeth said, "Another smooth flight and smoother landing. You are ruining me for commercial flights."

He chuckled and nodded. "And we almost beat the commercial flight time by two hours."

"And we thank you for that. As for the case, let's just say someone thinks Sherman Oaks is London's East End."

The pilot arched his eyebrows. "A Ripper copycat?"

"Great pilot *and* smart? If I wasn't involved with someone..."

The pilot burst into laughter. "Just my luck. However, I'm a happily married man." As she approached the front of the plane, he stepped back into the doorway of the cockpit to allow her room to pass. "Thanks for flying Alphabet Air."

"Can't beat the prices," Bobby said.

"And the scheduling," added Meredeth. She climbed down the built-in steps and turned her attention to the hangar. Two men stood near the human-sized door in the side of the building. L.A. County Homicide detectives, unless she missed her guess, almost wearing the unofficial uniforms of male plainclothes cops everywhere—comfortable shoes shined to a high gloss, wash-and-wear slacks in dark colors, belt, dress shirt and tie, and off-the-rack suit coat. Judging by the bulges, they also wore shoulder rigs to carry their primary weapons.

One of the detectives stepped forward, his hand outstretched in greeting. "Agent Connelly? I'm Cliff McCloe, Homicide for LASD. The big guy with the sour puss behind me is Roger Shelton, my partner."

Meredeth took his hand and gave it a firm squeeze. "Special Agent Meredeth Connelly, but I hope you'll dispense with formality and call me Meredeth. The Ken-doll making his way out of the plane is my partner, Bobby Van Zandt." She glanced at Roger, who was tall and heavily muscled...and also didn't seem too comfortable meeting her direct gaze.

"Meetcha," said Cliff as he raised his eyes to a point over and behind her right shoulder.

"Right back at you," said Bobby.

"Let's get out of this heat," grumbled Shelton. "We'll have our fill of it at the crime scene."

"Unless you don't care about the crime scene?" asked Cliff.

"No, I do," said Meredeth. "It helps me get a feel for the mind that committed the murder."

"That's settled then." Cliff raised his gaze to the Gulfstream and issued a low whistle. "Must be nice."

"It is," said Meredeth, "but we don't get to use it very often. My boss thought waiting until later this afternoon back home would lose us a day, so he wrangled us a ride."

"Car's this way," said Shelton as he turned and headed for the door. "It's not as luxurious as that G650, but then again, it can't lose power and drop out of the sky like a stone."

"Is he always this positive?" Meredeth stage whispered to Cliff.

"No," said Shelton over his shoulder. "Sometimes we catch a bad case, and then I get grumpy."

"It's true," said Cliff. "And if he doesn't get his morning donut and coffee, watch out."

"I'll bear that in mind," Meredeth said with a grin.

"Donuts do make me happy," said Roger. "So does closing cases. I don't suppose this one will go easy."

Meredeth shook her head and stepped out into the LA sunshine. "I hope you're wrong, but the realist inside me tends to agree. Tell me, are there other serial cases ongoing or suspected in L.A. County?"

Cliff shrugged. "A couple of cold cases and one with the last victim found three and a half weeks ago."

"We'll need to review those files, too," said Bobby.

"We'll generate profiles for all four cases, by the way. Maybe we can shake something loose on those cold cases and make Roger happy."

"If you can, then I'll buy you donuts for life," said the big cop.

"Deal," said Bobby.

The sunshine was glorious, but Meredeth started to feel like a dinner roll in the oven. She gestured at the ugly brown Crown Victoria that had seen many, many miles of hard use. "Is this you?"

"Nah, nah," said Shelton. "We're all modern and stuff." He pointed at a silver late-model Chevy Impala. "That's us right over there."

"Nice," said Bobby. "I guess it's not much for pursuits."

"That's a limited police version," said Shelton, a defensive note creeping into his voice. "Three hundred and two horsepower and decent gas mileage to boot. StabiliTrak, the works. It tops out at a buck-fifty."

"Not bad," said Bobby, sidling over to stand next to Shelton. "And I bet that's a great color for driving around in the sun."

"Sure, but the black interior makes it a little less so."

Bobby chuckled. "Bureaucrats, eh? I bet they got a deal on the jet black."

"You know it," grunted Shelton. "Let me get the air-conditioning running. You two will have to sit in the back, and that's vinyl, but at least we don't have a full cage back there."

"SOP," said Bobby. "We'll have a rental as soon as we go pick it up."

"We can handle that after you've seen the murder scene," said Cliff. "It's only twenty or so miles, but it'll take us the better part of an hour if the 405 is a parking lot."

Meredeth and Bobby shoved their bags into the trunk, then climbed into the back on opposite sides. "All set," Bobby said as he fastened his seat belt. The temperature in the car was a touch too warm to be comfortable, but cold air blew between the front buckets.

Roger left the parking lot and weaved his way onto the access road that circled the airport, then north on Sepulveda Boulevard to the Howard Hughes, and finally pointed the nose of the Impala up the I-405 on-ramp and accelerated to highway speed. Shelton drove fast but with care. There were some slowdowns, but they made good time—facilitated by their police light and a couple of blips from the siren. He took the Sepulveda exit, then turned right on Ventura Boulevard. "We think the vic took a shortcut. An alleyway across from Kindred Haven," he said. "It's more of a direct route to the hospital's temporary lot for the staff."

"Temporary?" asked Bobby. "How temporary?"

Cliff laughed. "Well, this is California. Worse, this is L.A. County, and Sherman Oaks, to boot. If it's not related to shopping, things sort of get stuck. The temporary lot has been there for... What, Rog, three years?"

"Sounds right."

"Why would she take the alley?"

Roger pumped his shoulders up and down. "Otherwise, she'd have to walk a couple of blocks east on Ventura, cross at the intersection of Stansbury Avenue, two more blocks to Dickens, then two blocks west to the temporary garage."

"Wait, the *temporary* lot is a concrete parking structure?" asked Bobby with a half-grin.

"Yeah," said Cliff. "It was standing empty when the apartment complex it supported went bust. The hospital leased the whole kit -and caboodle, empty apartments and all."

"Why do they need temporary parking in the first place?" asked Meredeth.

"There's a very small lot adjacent to the hospital for the doctors, and a small parking garage for visitors and patients. That leaves the nurses, orderlies, various technicians, and businesspeople out in the cold. Such as it is."

"And is the alley that deserted that—"

"Not at all. At least during the day. But at night, when the businesses across Ventura from the Kindred Haven are closed, the only traffic is on foot. The second half of the alley lies between two apartment complexes, but there are trees that block the view of the alley from above. I imagine that at night, it's blacker than pitch down there. That's where he took her, in the second half, but close to the middle of the alley."

"Here we are," said Roger. "Look to your left, half a block up. That big building is Kindred Haven Hospital."

"Good," said Meredeth. "I want to go there afterward. Let's see what kind of a person Mary Ann Blocker was."

Roger nodded and turned right into the alley between the Mercata Del Sole and something called William Keller Luxury International. The alley was paved and about twice the width of the Impala. Parking lots stood behind each building on Ventura—large, open paved lots, some with chain link fencing demarking their area, others with concrete walls and metal gates. Just past the lot behind

William Keller, a ramp descended into an underground garage with a metal-grid box protecting the entrance. And after that came the center point of the alley.

Shelton pulled into a wide-open area at the north end of the apartment building on the right and flipped down his visor, displaying the Los Angeles County Sheriff's Department badge and the words "On duty detectives" to combat the private parking signs. They got out and Meredeth walked to the crime scene tape strung across the alley from the back corner of each apartment building.

All in all, it was a nice alley—clean, groomed landscaping on either side, complete with juvenile birch and oak trees. The building on the left had individual parking garages on the ground floor and large, double-bay roll-up doors were the primary features. On the right, there were two iron gates securing a ground-floor parking garage. Each building had plenty of security, but above each garage door on the left was a security system box and a camera.

Meredeth pointed at the nearest camera. "Anyone working on the footage?"

"Yep," said Cliff. "Two guys from our tech department are helping the building's owner find them. The owner's not much on technology."

"Ah." Meredeth pointed into the long rectangle marked off by the yellow tape. "Can I go in?" There was a CSI van at the other end of the alley, but no one was visible. "Do you run a log?"

"Electronic," said Roger. "It works by GPS and registers our LASD phones."

"What about me?"

"I'll make a note for you two." He moved to the tape, lifted it, and ducked under.

"Can I walk the scene alone for a few minutes?" asked Meredeth.

Roger cocked his head to the side, giving her an amused look. "I thought that was an invention of Hollywood scriptwriters. You really do that?"

Meredeth grinned. "Maybe I saw one too many Thomas Harris movies when I was a kid."

"Or that movie with Ethan Hawke and Angelina Jolie."

"Oh, I loved that one," said Cliff. "*Taking Lives* it was called. But they didn't get much right in terms of the procedures. Unless cops in Canada do things differently."

"I doubt it," said Roger. "Here." He lifted the yellow tape and motioned for Meredeth to pass underneath. "The scene's all yours, but if I catch you lying in the chalk outline, you're buying lunch and dinner."

Meredeth laughed brightly. "I don't go that far." Shelton nodded, and she stepped past him. Her eyes went to the blood splatter three feet in front of her, and she moved around to the other side of it, standing facing the two cops and Bobby. She lifted her left hand and made a sweeping slice from her right to left. She glanced down at the blood splatter and furrowed her brow. The angle wasn't quite right, and she moved to her left and turned so she would've faced the victim on a forty-five-degree angle. "He rushed the initial blow."

"He probably stood back there in the shadows, maybe behind those shrubs." McCloe pointed at one of the concrete block pillars that stood to either side of the closest garage door and the manicured shrub that hid the pillar from sight.

Meredeth nodded, then shifted her attention back to the blood splatter. Another arc was a few steps away, but it wasn't the blood splatter caused by another blow of the knife—it wasn't uniform enough. "She fought him. Right there." She pointed at the sloppy spots and streaks of brown on the asphalt, then followed the trail of blood that meandered back and forth before disappearing into one of the planting beds at the base of the building to the right. On the wall above that bed, the killer had used her blood to paint "Eight little whores" in foot-high letters. Below it, he'd written "No hope of heaven." She pointed at the bed. "That's where she fell and bled out. He watched, maybe sitting astride her to keep her from attempting another run to the mouth of the alley."

"That's what we figured, too," said Cliff.

Meredeth nodded and advanced toward the planting bed and the red-stained low ground cover. "He made the rest of the marks postmortem. He wanted to get them right, to make them perfect." She glanced up at the letters on the wall. "And even so, he still messed up the quote."

"Quote?" asked Roger.

Meredeth nodded. "It's a quote from a poem sent to the police in 1888. The poem was allegedly penned by Jack the Ripper. The next line says, 'Gladstone may save one, then there'll be seven.' I guess he didn't want to give you any ideas about saving one."

"We don't need a disgusting poem for that," said Cliff.

"No, I don't suppose you do." She squatted on her hunkers, staring down at the tape outline of Mary Ann Blocker's body. To either side, the ground cover was smashed into the dirt as if someone knelt there and shifted his weight around until he ground the plant into the soil. "He straddled her to mutilate her." She moved her intense gaze back and forth across the bed in a grid, looking for something the killer might have left behind but only found blood. "Did he mutilate her?"

"Beyond the lacerations? No," said Roger.

"No missing organs?"

"Nothing like that."

Meredeth nodded and pursed her lips. Then she stood and walked toward the other end of the alley, her gaze on the ground, scanning from wall to wall. She hoped to find more blood transferred by the unsub but found nothing, so she turned back and repeated the process all the way to where Bobby, Cliff, and Roger stood. "Not much here," she said as she came closer. "Just the blood and the abused plant life. Did your CSI teams find anything else?"

Cliff shook his head. "Not that they've communicated to us. The ME might have something for us later this afternoon, but most likely it will be a day or two."

Meredeth sucked her teeth.

CHAPTER 6

KINDRED SOULS

Sherman Oaks, CA

MEREDETH WATCHED CARS zipping by on Ventura Boulevard for a moment. "You said she would have crossed from the hospital, then come down this alley? I'd like to trace her route back to the hospital. Perhaps the unsub followed her from the hospital and caught her up back there." She waved a lackadaisical hand behind her.

"Wouldn't she have heard him?" asked Cliff.

"Yes," said Bobby, "unless the man is some kind of ninja. Or maybe David Carradine."

"She may have heard him, sped up, and that's why he rushed the first strike," said Meredeth. "At any rate, it *is* unlikely, but I'd like to exclude it based on the evidence rather than assume it didn't happen. The businesses up there might have security cameras. If we can verify she was alone on Ventura, I think we can solidify the theory that he lay in wait."

Roger nodded. "Sounds like a plan. Plus, Kindred Haven isn't far. Two blocks, give or take." He turned and strode off toward the Ventura mouth of the alley, and the others followed him, walking in a straight line: Cliff McCloe on Meredeth's left, and Bobby on her right. They walked with their heads down, focused on the alley's pavement, looking for anything that might give them a clue—blood, scuff marks from a person on foot, cast-off or dropped items—but as with the other end of the alley, there was nothing to see.

They turned right, walking by the Mercata Del Sole and its sister business, Trattoria Del Sole. Meredeth pointed at the door. "Bobby? Check for inside cameras with a view of the street."

"Aye-aye, boss," he said as he moved to the door and entered the building.

Meredeth watched as he approached the counter and made the twenty-something taking orders laugh aloud. He showed her his badge, and her face grew somber. Then, she shook her head, and Meredeth turned to the next building, which was standing empty. She turned her attention to the building across the street. She raised her hand and pointed. "There," she said. "Camera over the door."

"I'll check it out and meet you at the hospital," said Roger. Then he jogged across the four-lane road and walked inside the brick and concrete building.

Bobby exited Trattoria Del Sole and shook his head. "No cameras."

"Roger's checking across the street," said Cliff. "He'll catch up to us at Kindred Home—which might also have external cameras that cover Ventura."

"We'll ask," said Meredeth.

"Let's cross," said Cliff, looking for oncoming traffic from the west. He started across the street, and the two FBI agents followed.

Kindred Haven was a smaller hospital, with only five floors for the main building, though some of the specialty buildings located on the block across Calhoun Avenue were taller. Two concrete pillars supported a header over the ambulance entrance for the ER. The main building architecture was old—a product of the sixties or seventies, with windows reaching from the ground to the second floor, followed by a half wall and more windows, and that pattern repeated to the roof. The entrance was inset a little, boasting double powered glass doors.

They entered the main lobby, and Meredeth approached the information desk. "Hello," she said to the attendant. "My name is Special Agent Meredeth Connelly. LASD has requested our assistance with respect to the incident in the alley across the street. We need to speak to Mary Ann Blocker's co-workers."

"Nurses only or do you want doctors, too?"

"Everyone."

"That could be an issue. Ms. Blocker was a scrub nurse."

"Why would that be an issue?"

"She worked the OR, with any surgeons or anesthetists who happened to be scheduled. Finding every doctor she's worked with will require getting the scheduling records from HR, then the surgical schedule for the ORs she was assigned to."

"I see."

"But I could see if Dr. Gull can speak to you. He's the head of surgery."

"That would be great. While you're working on that, can we speak with the other OR nurses?"

The woman nodded. "The operating rooms are on the fifth floor. Look for the red stripe on the floor that says 'Do not enter.' There's a yellow phone on the wall. Pick that up and tell them you need to speak to nurses who worked with Mary Ann. There's a waiting room nearby that you can use to conduct your interviews."

"Thanks. Here, take my card. You can text me about the chief of surgery." She handed over one of her business cards with a smile, then turned back to Cliff and Bobby. As she walked toward them, Roger strode into the lobby and gave her a nod. "She's checking on the chief of surgery, but we can go up and interview the OR nurses who worked with the vic."

"Good," said Roger. "Fourth floor, if I recall correctly."

"Fifth," said Meredeth as she turned and looked for an elevator. "We're to find the red stripe on the ground then

pick up the yellow phone nearby and tell them what we
need."

CHAPTER 7
CATCHING A CHILL
David Branch's Farm, NY

CARL TRIED KEEPING his expression neutral as he watched Lucy flirting with the new kid—a guy named Jack. She stood next to Jack, laughing at every joke he told, gazing up at him with rapt attention. In other words, doing everything but wearing a blinking neon sign that said, "I like you. Want to noodle?"

Carl gritted his teeth and sniffed. He wasn't sure what was worse, being manipulated but having someone he could rely on to be there, someone he could get into bed on a moment's notice, or not being manipulated and watching her go after someone else. "I don't care who she likes," he muttered. "She can get with anyone she wants."

He considered leaving the room, but then he caught it—Lucy laughed at another joke, running her hand down Jack's arm from his bicep to his wrist but glancing at Carl out of the corner of her eye as she did so. He ducked his head to hide the smile. He was on to her. *She's trying to make me jealous. More manipulation.*

With that last thought came a surge of anger that nearly overwhelmed his self-control. He set his face in a cold expression of disapproval and pushed himself away from the rough-hewn planking that made up the barn's outer walls. He turned away from the house and walked away. Lucy's loud, rolling laughter followed him up the hill.

At the crown of the hill, he paused and glanced back—Lucy was staring at him, poor Jack ignored and confused for the moment. When she saw him looking, she turned her attention back to Jack, then stood on her tiptoes and kissed the boy on the cheek.

Carl turned and walked toward Mack's Peterbilt, even though the hood was closed and neither Father nor Mack seemed to be around. The tractor Jonathon had started working on sat outside, next to the Pete, parts strewn around it on the ground. He grimaced and approached the old tractor, trying to make heads or tails of whatever Jonathon had been doing—which appeared to be taking off random accessories and laying them in the dirt at his feet.

Shaking his head, Carl got to work putting the thing back together. It was good to have his hands on something he could fix. It took his attention, keeping his mind busy so he didn't have to reconsider the same old arguments about Lucy for the six-millionth time since lunch.

"Hey," said a female voice.

Carl straightened and turned his back to the tractor. Michelina stood near the trees on the crown of the hill. She was tall and pretty. Blonde where Lucy was brunette, with blue eyes so light they were almost gray. She was older than Lucy and was losing that "high school girl" look in favor of the "college girl" look in his estimation—though Carl had never seen either. "Hey, yourself."

"I don't see you and Lucy hanging out much anymore."

"No, you don't, and what's more, you won't."

"Ah," she said and walked toward him. "What did she do?"

Carl shook his head once, then sniffed. "She's too manipulative."

"Oh?"

He nodded. "Just watch her try to make me jealous with that new kid."

"Jack?"

"That's the one. She's waving her floozy flag, coming on to him in such an obvious manner, but every now and again, she checks to make sure I'm watching."

"Ew," said Michelina. "That sounds icky."

"Yeah," he said with a sigh. He bent and picked up the tractor's alternator and shook his head. "I don't know what the hell Jonathon was doing here."

The blonde girl chuckled. "Oh, that's easy. Father kept sending him away while he, you, and Mack worked. Finally, Father said he could work on the tractor—probably just to get rid of him. He pulled the tractor out so he could eavesdrop on your conversations."

"Oh. What an asshat. If I hadn't already cut out his heart, I'd consider knocking out his teeth."

Michelina laughed, but it sounded forced to Carl's ears.

"So, what are you doing up here?" he asked.

"Taking a walk. The house gets so noisy when Father's away, and I have to take breaks from all the noobs."

Carl nodded and shrugged an eyebrow. "Yeah, the youngsters get so..."

"*Exactly*," said Michelina with a bell-like laugh. "I get so tired of hanging out with *children*. I want to spend time with *adults* once in while at least."

"What about Mack?" he asked.

"What about him?" she countered, stopping about six feet from him, and grasping her hands behind her back.

Carl couldn't help but notice how that one move seemed to make her breasts stand at attention. They were perfect, as far as he could tell with the knit top she wore. "Why haven't we spent time together?"

Again, she rolled out the chiming laughter. "Lucy."

"Ah, yeah." Carl smiled, and Michelina smiled back. "But you never answered me."

"About Mack?"

Carl nodded.

"I like him, there's no doubt, but he's too consumed with his plans to pay much attention... Not like you paid attention to Lucy."

Carl found a rag and wiped the grease from his fingers. "You mind company on your walk?"

Michelina smiled. "Not at all, as long as the company is you."

A one-sided smile twisted his lips. "Then let's go."

"Maybe we can find a secluded spot to...have a chat."

"I'd like that," Carl said, feeling a pleasant stirring in his loins. "I know a place in the woods—lots of pine needles to make the ground comfortable, and the canopy opens up as if to give a good view of the sky. We could stay until after dark, maybe look at the sky."

"Or maybe do it again after dark." She wore a come-hither expression and a smile.

"I'd..." He had to swallow hard to get some moisture in his mouth. "I'd like that."

She held out her hand, and he took it.

Neither of them saw Lucy watching from the corner of the machine shed.

CHAPTER 8

GOWN AND GLOVES

Sherman Oaks, CA

THE ELEVATOR DISGORGED the four of them into a blinding-white hallway that ran straight away from the elevator. Unlike the lobby, and, Meredeth assumed, the other floors of the hospital, there were no decorations, no plants, no festive little signs to tell you that your symptoms might be cancer or Ebola or some other biblical plague. Similarly, the flooring was white linoleum rather than the soft-blue gray tiles in the lobby.

There was no chance of getting lost, though, given that there was only one hallway stretching away from the elevator. Up ahead, the hallway dead-ended at a T-shaped intersection, and opposite the hall they stood in, Meredeth spotted the surgical waiting room the receptionist had said they could use for their interview—and like the hall, it was spartan, though comfortable looking—but she didn't see a red line or a yellow phone. "Maybe on one of the arms of the T," she murmured.

"Yeah," said Cliff. "You go right for the ORs, left for the recovery room and surgical critical care ward."

"Ah," she said. "Thanks." She began walking toward the intersection, and the men fell in behind them.

"Any strategy you want to run when we interview the nurses?"

"Not really," said Meredeth. "Just follow my lead. My assumption for each person we interview is that they are witnesses until one of us spots something that puts them in the suspect category."

"We should have some kind of code word," said Cliff. "Like 'manatee,' or we could say something like: 'That's not the impression Dr. X left me with.'"

"Manatee?" asked Bobby.

"Sure. It's not like anyone would interject the word by mistake."

"I'll give you that..."

"Why don't we just use trattoria, like the tavern across the street," said Meredeth. "If your radar or internal lie detectors go off, suggest we stop by the Trattoria Del Sole to grab a bite."

"Sounds good," said Roger, and Bobby nodded his agreement.

"I still think 'Dr. X' or 'manatee' would work just fine, but I'll go along."

They rounded the corner and saw the red stripe of linoleum across white. Above it hung the promised yellow phone.

Meredeth strode over to the phone and picked up the handset. "Hm. No dial pad," she said.

"It's a direct connection, ma'am. This is the OR nurses' station. Is there something I can do for you?"

"I'm Special Agent Meredeth Connelly. I'm here with my partner, Special Agent Van Zandt, and two homicide detectives from LASD. We'd—"

"Oh, my," said the nurse.

"—like to talk to friends and coworkers of Mary Ann Blocker."

"The poor girl! Of course, we want to help, but please understand that nurses can't step away from an OR. We'll have to grab them between surgeries."

"That would be fine. Is anyone available now?"

"Yes. A few are charting their last surgery. I'll send someone out with surgical gowns and gloves for you to put on. It gets a little warm, but it really is necessary."

"For sterility. Sure, we understand," said Meredeth, "but we can have our chats in the waiting room. That way we don't risk contamination."

"Oh, sure. I'll send Liz Pacer out first."

"That will be fine. Thank you. Will we be able to speak with you, as well?"

"If you think it will help, of course. I just need someone to watch the desk for me."

"See if you can arrange that while we speak with Ms. Pacer."

"Will do."

"Good. Talk soon." Meredeth hung up and turned to face the men. She twirled her finger in the air, telling them to turn around. "Back to that waiting room."

They retraced their steps back to the T-intersection and stepped into the waiting room there. An attempt to soften the harsh sterility of the hallways had been made in the waiting room. The walls were soft yellow, and the floor had been tiled with a tan, distressed porcelain. An area rug and four full-length couches and a bevy of armchairs created a sort of conversation pit, though Meredeth couldn't imagine anyone striking up a full conversation in the room.

She moved one of the armchairs into the center of the rug, pointed at Bobby at the sofa to the chair's left. She directed Cliff and Roger at the couch facing the chair. For her own part, she didn't intend to sit. She wanted to be mobile. She wanted to remain silent. "Bobby, you conduct the interview. However, if we plan lunch, I'll step in."

"What would you like us to do?" asked Cliff.

"Feel free to interject questions as they arise, but remember these aren't suspects, so go easy."

The two detectives glanced at one another, then nodded.

"I'll make them nervous, I have no doubt," she said. "Let's plan on exploiting that to dig a little deeper than we otherwise might."

"Sounds like a plan."

"Good, because our first witness is probably halfway here, already."

They settled in and put their game faces on. Meredeth moved over to the entrance but did not step out into the hall.

CHAPTER 9
LIZ PACER, RN
Sherman Oaks, CA

A PETITE WOMAN with jet black hair and a light complexion rounded the corner into the surgical waiting room, almost running right into Meredeth. She jumped back, one hand pressed to her chest. "Good gravy, you gave me a start!"

Meredeth said nothing, only smiled and motioned the woman toward the conversation pit. After the woman stepped past her, she followed a little too close, just on the edge of the woman's personal space.

The woman hesitated a moment, gazing back and forth between the LASD detectives and Van Zandt, but then sat and smoothed her scrubs with nervous hands. Meredeth stepped onto the area rug just outside the nurse's cone of vision, then paced to the other end of the rug.

"Hello," said Cliff, "I'm Detective Clifford McCloe, and this is my partner, Roger Shelton. The rugged guy to your left is Special Agent Van Zandt, and the woman pacing behind you is Special Agent Meredeth Connelly. Both work for the FBI's BAU—do you know what that means?"

"Of course," said the nurse, "I watched Criminal Minds just like the rest of America. But..."

"But why are the FBI involved?" asked Bobby with his winning smile and laugh lines appearing around his eyes. "There are certain aspects of the crime that warrant our expertise, and the LASD requested our assistance."

"Oh." The woman shifted in her seat, throwing a glance behind her but to the wrong side. "Mary Ann was a sweetheart. I can't understand why anyone would want her dead."

"Before we get into the questions, can you give us your name and contact information?" Roger passed his investigator's notepad across to her along with his pen.

"Sorry. I'm Liz Pacer."

"Are you a nurse or..." said Bobby, quirking his eyebrows.

Liz glanced at him and nodded. "Yes, I'm a registered nurse, just like Mary Ann."

"And you're a scrub nurse?" asked Roger.

"Yes, I am. I have been for nearly ten years."

"I see. And you worked with Mary Ann Blocker?"

"I did, but our relationship eclipsed the work-friend status almost immediately. We had so much in common, so many shared interests."

"Can you tell us about Mary Ann?" Bobby asked.

"She was a good nurse. She really cared, you know? And not just about patients and their families. She cared about her co-workers, she cared about the surgeons, the anesthesiologists, but she also really cared about the support staff—you know, the techs, the janitors, the maintenance men, everyone, really. When she was out of the OR, she was never too busy to help or to talk, and that extended from doctors down to janitors. *Everyone* liked her these days." She shook her head. "Why did this happen? Who killed her? Was she raped?"

"We can't give you those answers," said Bobby. "Some because we don't know the answers—"

"Yet," said Meredeth, and Liz startled and turned to look at her.

"—and some because we can't share information about an ongoing investigation. Was there anyone who paid too much or simply the wrong kind of attention to her? Anyone who hung out to catch her alone or to walk her to her car?"

"Not that I ever noticed, and not that she told me about."

"She worked very late the night of her murder. Do you have any idea why?"

"Surgeries don't always go to plan," Liz said. "Once we're in an OR with a patient opened up on the table, we stay until the work is done. Everyone does, from the surgery techs to the surgeons themselves."

"Ah. Any idea what surgery kept her?"

"I can't tell you the patient's name or any medical details, but it was a trauma surgery that came up from the emergency room at the last minute. Mary Ann volunteered to stay and help out."

"Ah. Then she wasn't scheduled to work that late. Did she frequently stay late?"

"I suppose. We all try to, as we get time and a half for those surgeries because they happen outside of our normal hours, and since we volunteer to stay past our ten-hour shift, we get another half—double time, in other words."

"Ah, good money?" asked Cliff.

"Sure. Scrub nurses make a little more than your typical RN, so double time can really add up."

"How often do you stay late?" asked Roger.

"Every chance I get...though I suppose that will have to change until Kindred Haven can offer us secure parking."

"That sounds wise," said Bobby. "If I understand you, it was difficult to dislike Mary Ann. Did anyone rise to the challenge?"

Liz shrugged. "Look, Mary Ann wasn't perfect. No one is, right?"

"Correct," said Meredeth, eliciting another jump from Liz and another quick glance over the woman's shoulder. "Give us an example of her imperfection."

"Sh-sure. Her work was exceptional, and that did ruffle some feathers from the lazier nurses, but over time, they were encouraged to switch departments and most of them did, and the staff now looks—*looked*—up to Mary Ann as someone to emulate."

"Encouraged to leave by whom?" asked Cliff.

"Dr. Gull, the chief of surgery."

"Why?" asked Bobby. "Isn't the devil you know better than the one you don't?"

"He runs a tight department," said Liz. "He's raised our stats by a significant amount as he demands excellence from everyone. When he took the appointment three years ago, some of the scrub nurses left a lot to be desired and comparing them to a nurse like Mary Ann made their failures glaringly obvious."

"And some of them were grumpy about the comparison?"

"Sure," said Liz with a shrug. "Like I said, scrub nurses make more than ward nurses."

"I see," said Bobby. "But this Dr. Gull liked Mary Ann?"

"Ha!" she scoffed. "I'm not sure Dr. Gull likes anyone. He's opinionated and sure he's right about everything. He's a bit of an M. Deity."

"M. Deity?"

"Right. M.D.—medical doctor. M. Deity—medical doctor with a God complex."

"Ah, I see."

"The thing about Mary Ann is that once a flaw or something she overlooked was pointed out to her, she fixed the problem and made sure she never caused another like it. She was very conscientious. Committed."

"And Dr. Gull appreciated her work ethic?"

"If he even noticed her work ethic, he said nothing. It's not his way. But what he would have noticed was that she wasn't coming onto his radar. She wasn't making the same mistake, again and again." She pursed her lips and glanced up and to the right. "And perhaps that's his way of expressing approval—ignoring you."

"Sounds like a great boss," said Bobby with a faint smile.

"Shut up, you," said Meredeth with a faux growl.

"Uh, yeah, but Dr. Gull isn't really our boss. I mean, he is, because he's in charge of the surgery department, not to mention that he's a doctor, but the nursing staff has their own chain of command."

Bobby nodded. "What else can you tell us about Mary Ann? Was she dating?"

"No, I don't think she was dating anyone in particular lately. Like I said before, she is—was—a very caring individual, but outside of work, she showed her sarcastic side. She could be sharp-tongued."

"What did she do for fun?" asked Cliff.

"Well..." Liz dropped her gaze to her lap.

Meredeth stepped around the chair and squatted in front of her, resting a hand on her knee. "You're a good friend, Liz, and I'm sure Mary Ann appreciated your reluctance to speak about her private life."

"But?"

"But she's gone, now, and I'm sure she'd want you to help us find the jerk that ambushed her and took her life."

Liz nodded and met Meredeth's gaze. "I'm sure you're correct. People sometimes get the wrong idea—a pretty, single woman, and all. There have been rumors about Mary Ann's promiscuity."

"Everything you say to us, we'll use only to lock up the unsub," said Bobby. "We don't judge, we just consider the information and use it if we can."

"She liked to have fun. She liked sex."

"And since she wasn't in a relationship..."

Liz nodded. "We'd go out to a club, and nine times out of ten, she didn't need a ride home, if you know what I mean."

"I do," said Meredeth with a solemn nod. "And her interest was men?"

"Oh! Yes, absolutely. Mary Ann and I were just friends."

"Of course. I never thought differently."

"I mean, we were close, and there have been occasional rumors that she and I... Well, you know. *Unfounded* rumors."

"Yes," said Meredeth. "These clubs you went to...did she have any favorites? Did she ever leave with the same man more than once?"

"She may have. I really didn't pay attention."

"Didn't it make you angry?" asked Roger.

"Angry?"

"Yeah, that you'd go out with Mary Ann, and she'd ditch you for some guy?"

Liz chuckled. "No. Those guys were kind of the point of going to a loud club, right? For both of us."

"I see."

"How about at the clubs? Did she attract the wrong sort of attention there? Did you catch men watching her or paying her too much attention?"

Liz chuckled, again. "Like I said, getting guys was the point. We didn't wear our scrubs."

"Oh? How did you dress?"

"Miniskirts, shorts, tight pants. There were a lot of people who stared at Mary Ann. She was beautiful when she put her mind to it." She frowned. "That came out wrong. All I meant is that when she wanted to, she could look like an underwear model."

"I see," said Bobby. "And no one ever bothered her? No one sent drinks after she'd told them to buzz off?"

"No, nothing like that."

Bobby shifted his gaze to Meredeth. "How about her neighbors or ex-boyfriends?" she asked. "Did she get the wrong kind of attention?"

"No," said Liz, shaking her head sadly. "Her ex initiated the divorce, and from what Mary Ann said, it was amicable."

Meredeth glanced at Cliff and arched her eyebrows. He shook his head, and she repeated the process with Roger, who reacted the same way. "I want to thank you for your candor, Liz. Can we contact you in the future if we need to clarify something you've said?"

"Of course. Any time."

Roger stood and blew out a long breath. "I need a break."

"Already?" asked Cliff. "We'll grab a bite when we're done here."

"It's not that," said Roger, walking to the hall. "Did anyone see a bathroom?"

CHAPTER 10

THE BIG TIME

Sherman Oaks, CA

ON HIS PHONE, Druitt scanned the Los Angeles Daily News. The murder took the headline, and the story had an Associated Press link showing it had gone national. That made him smile a little.

The story itself didn't contain much accuracy, but since the LASD hadn't made a statement about the crime yet, he didn't expect much more. They had the alley right, but the rest of the so-called "facts of the crime" were simply wild-ass guesses. He read on, skimming through the bits about Mary Ann's life, but when he reached the paragraph immediately following that, he grimaced.

"The Los Angeles County Sheriff's Department has requested the aid of criminal profilers from the Federal Bureau of Investigations Behavioral Science Unit—to wit, superprofiler pair, Senior Special Agent Meredeth Connelly, and her partner, Special Agent Robert Van Zandt."

Despite the iron control over his emotions that he prided himself on, a shiver of fear raced through him when he read Connelly's name in print. He knew her, had studied her methods, her cases, and knew she was an opponent worthy of his respect and careful attention.

He leaned back, his gaze going distant, his hands dropping to his lap, automatically pressing the lock button on his private phone. He hadn't expected the FBI's involvement. Not yet, not until his third victim, at least. But he *had* planned on the eventuality, and the early attention only meant he had to enact his plans sooner than he'd expected. *Damn the LASD!* he thought.

A faint grin settled on his lips, and the sliver of fear turned into anticipation of a good hunt. He leaned forward and printed the article on his office laser jet, then trimmed the edges with scissors and slid it into his laptop case so he'd remember to take it home.

CHAPTER 11

MILDRED McFADDEN, LPN

Sherman Oaks, CA

THE NEXT PERSON who walked into their make-shift interview room was Mildred McFadden, the person to whom Meredeth had spoken on the intercom phone. She gave her name—Mildred McFadden, who had already given her contact information to Roger Shelton in the hall as he returned from his break—and took her seat in the middle of the arrayed couches.

Meredeth dispensed with the "pacing behind her" routine and perched on the edge of the couch opposite Bobby. The seating arrangement ensured that one of them would always have the freedom to observe McFadden without her knowing.

"Ms. McFadden, these men—"

"Call me 'Mildred,' dear."

"Very well," said Meredeth. "Mildred, as I said on the telephone, my name is Meredeth Connelly, and I'm with the FBI. The G.I. Joe across from me is Bobby Van Zandt, my partner. The two men in front of you are LASD Homicide detectives, Clifford McCloe and Roger Shelton."

McFadden nodded to each man as Meredeth introduced them.

"As you know, we're looking into Mary Ann Blocker's death."

"Yes. I'm not sure how I can help. I liked Mary Ann, but we weren't contemporaries, and we didn't socialize outside of work. Here at the hospital, she was as sweet as can be, but I heard rumors about her sharp tongue and her...*lifestyle*."

"What are you referring to?" asked Bobby.

"She was what we once called 'a loose woman.' Do you know what I mean by that?"

"Isn't that a faux-polite way of calling her a slut?" asked Meredeth.

"I want to make this clear," said Mildred. "Personally, I've never understood the double standard in our culture. If this hot young man sleeps with a new girl every night, he's celebrated, but a hot young woman is a slut, a bimbo. I don't really care what Mary Ann did in her private life, I'm just passing on what I've heard reputable *women* say about her lifestyle."

"I see, but you have no direct knowledge of it?"

"No," said Mildred shaking her head.

"That's fine, but for now, let's stick to what you know by direct observation or experience."

"Okay. Mary Ann was an incredible nurse. In fact, she was so good, most people around here thought it was a loss when she moved to the surgery team. Well, except the doctors, they're all happy. As a co-worker, she was incredible. She was always happy to help provided she wasn't tasked with something else."

"How did she interact with the staff?"

"Always pleasant, even when those nasty rumors were floating around. When she had the time—that is to say, when she wasn't assisting in a surgery—she was always happy to talk to anyone. She was very supportive—regardless of the other person's position here at the hospital."

"Even with the doctors?"

"Of course."

"And with the other nurses?"

"Yes, these days."

"These days?"

"Well, when Dr. Gull became the chief of surgery, he wasn't happy with the quality of work coming out of the scrub and circulating nurses. He found them lazy or incompetent." She frowned. "I want to tell you he wasn't always right. He tends to make snap judgments and won't reassess those judgments, even in light of overwhelming evidence that he was wrong. He decided that most of the surgical staff needed to switch to another role in the hospital."

"Yes, Liz mentioned that."

"I see. Did she also tell you that he held Mary Ann up as an example of the kind of scrub nurse he was interested in employing? He repeated that often, and it made a lot of people bitter or angry. Some of those nurses took things out on Mary Ann despite the fact that she really had nothing to do with it, except that she was a great nurse."

"Did any of those bitter or angry nurses carry things too far?"

Mildred pursed her lips and looked at the ceiling. "Not really, no. I mean, people griped and groaned, but..."

"How about white males between twenty and forty? Any nurses fit in that category that were fired?"

"Oh, no one was fired. They were *encouraged* to find another department to move over to."

"Sure. Any white males in that age range encouraged to move along?"

"Two," said Mildred. " and Walt Segart."

"I see. Do they still work at Kindred Haven?"

"Aaron definitely does. I saw him just last week. I'm not sure about Walt Segart."

"We'll find out," said Meredeth. "Anyone else you can think of? Perhaps one of the female nurses with a boyfriend or husband who was angry at their treatment from Dr. Gull?"

"I'm sure there were some, but I heard nothing one way or another."

"I see," said Meredeth. "You're the unit secretary for the OR suite?"

"And the recovery room."

"Let's talk about patients. Now"—Meredeth held up her hand, palm toward McFadden—"I don't care about names or medical details. Did any of the patients Mary Ann Blocker worked on have a bad or unexpected outcome of their surgery?"

"Dr. Gull will have to answer that question. I'm not comfortable speaking about patients."

"That isn't a no, Mildred," said Bobby with a smile.

"Maybe," she said with a shrug, "but it's also not a yes."

CHAPTER 12

M. DEITY

Sherman Oaks, CA

AS MILDRED MCFADDEN stood to leave, Meredeth's phone danced a jig in her jacket pocket, and she pulled it out and read the text message. "It seems Dr. Aaron Gull is ready to talk, and he invites us to swing by his office in the next fifteen minutes."

"Fifteen minutes?" asked Bobby.

"Well, he's *important*," said Meredeth with a grin.

"I guess the real question we should be asking ourselves is, where is his office?" asked Cliff.

"Always thinking, this one," said Roger in a gruff voice. He pushed himself up from the couch and stepped toward the hall. "Come on. Dr. Gull is right here on five."

Cliff also stood. "You know him?"

"Nah, nah," said Shelton. "But I did look him up in the hospital directory online. His office is 5053."

"Tall *and* resourceful," said Cliff, hooking his thumb at his partner. "Lead on, oh digital sage."

Roger rolled his eyes but moved out into the hall and turned in the opposite direction from the red line and yellow phone. "It's this way." He walked down the hall, taking it on faith that the others would follow—and he was right.

They reached 5053 in less than a minute as it was only ten doors away from the waiting room; however, the door was closed. Roger lifted his hand and banged on the wooden door. "Dr. Gull?" he called.

"Come!" The male voice was muted as though the office had sound-reducing insulation behind the sheetrock.

Roger turned the knob and stepped inside. They all fit inside the doctor's office, and once inside, it became obvious as to why: he'd had the wall between 5053 and 5055 removed to double his office space. His desk was perpendicular to the outside wall, in the section that had once been 5055.

"Dr. Gull? My name is Roger Shelton, and I'm a homicide detective with LASD. This is my partner, Cliff McCloe"—he twitched his thumb in Cliff's direction—"and these two are FBI. BAU to be precise. Meredeth Connelly and Bobby Van Zandt."

Dr. Gull rose to his feet, and he was at least as tall as Roger Shelton, though he lacked the other man's bulk. Also like Roger, his hair and eyes were dark, though he eschewed the crew cut Roger wore. His hair fell to his shoulders, a little wavy. He wasn't clean-shaven, nor did he have a beard, but instead, he had stubble somewhere in between. His gaze flicked first to Meredeth, then scanned across the three men and returned to her. "Nice to meet you all," he said. "I understand you're here at Kindred Haven today looking for background information on poor Mary Ann Blocker."

"That's right," said Cliff.

"Well, come in, come in. Sit wherever you are comfortable. I'm happy to assist if I can, though I have to say upfront that I didn't know Mary Ann socially."

"That's fine," said Meredeth. She crossed through where the wall had once stood and took a seat in front of Dr. Gull's desk. "Any detail might be helpful. Sometimes the smallest thing can break a case wide open."

"I find your chosen profession very interesting. I fix things. I *cure* cancer or any number of conditions that can lead to the casket, but to do so, I need concrete, *observable* symptoms. You, on the other hand, deal with one of the most obscure things known to modern medicine."

"The mind," said Bobby.

"That, too, but what I was thinking of was the human heart. Not the organ, mind you."

"You make a distinction between heart and mind?" asked Meredeth.

"Certainly. Don't you?"

"Only in as much as the term 'heart' tends to be associated with strong emotion—even though that is technically the domain of the mind."

"Yes, yes," said Gull, dropping his gaze to the blotter on his desk. For a moment, Meredeth thought he'd looked irritated, but when he raised his head, he was smiling. "Ah...forgive me. In my line of work, people who visit this office already know me—at least as much as doctor-patient relationships allow. My name is Aaron William Gull. As I alluded to, I'm a surgeon—Kindred Haven Hospital's Chief of Surgery as a matter of fact. The youngest in the hospital's history."

Meredeth examined his face closely. He had wrinkles around his eyes, and the skin under his jaw sagged a little like baby jowls that hadn't grown into their fullness yet. She flicked a glance at his hair, looking for gray, and found some strands, though not many. "Mid-thirties when you were appointed?"

"Very good, Agent Connelly. When you retire, you could get a job at the fair—those guys who guess ages and weights."

She looked him over once more. "I'd say one ninety to two hundred pounds."

Gull laughed, but Meredeth didn't think it reached his eyes. "Very good, Agent—"

"Please call me Meredeth."

"Meredeth, then. Good guess, though I weighed in at two-thirteen this morning. Then again, I'd think such skills are very useful in your line of work."

"Indeed," said Meredeth.

"How do you do it?" Gull asked as he sank into his desk chair after motioning the men to sit.

"Do what? Guess age and weight?"

"No, no," he said, and his lips twisted into a half smile. "I mean how do you—without even meeting them—wiggle your way into a killer's mind and figure out how he thinks?

Meredeth nodded, wagging her head from side to side. "It really isn't like what you see on television or in the movies. There's no ESP, no psychic connection, or anything like that. I imagine it's very similar to how you make a diagnosis. There are clues to any killer's mindset that can be extracted from the crime scene, from the ME's report. And we take a patient history of a sort—in part, what we are doing here today—but also from past crimes. And, like you, we start with some general assumptions and let the unsub's behavior inform our thinking as we narrow things down."

"But I can examine my patients directly, and then there are the machines that aid my diagnostic capabilities."

"Sure, but the machines and blood tests are akin to the clues we can extract from the physical evidence left at crime scenes, both current and past. And in some cases, killers can't resist sending us letters or notes, even marks cut into the flesh of decedents. You can view those like a direct examination of the patient. Handwriting, the cogency of the writing, even the pen choice can tell us things about the writer."

"And in Mary Ann's case?"

"I'm afraid I can't discuss those details at the present time."

"No, of course not." Gull leaned forward and steepled his fingers in front of his face, resting his elbows on his blotter. "Well, how can I help you?"

Meredeth had caught the flicker of annoyance when she declined to share details with the doctor, and if pressed, would have said his forward-leaning posture smacked of aggression. "Tell us about Mary Ann."

"She was a scrub nurse. A very *good* scrub nurse. I frequently asked for her when scheduling OR times. "

"What set her apart from the other scrub nurses?"

Gull tilted his head to the left and glanced upward. "Work ethic, for one. She did so much above and beyond her job description. Half her time was spent helping other nurses—even doctors. And her work was always done on time." He pursed his lips. "And I think she knew the surgical procedures as well as anyone can who hasn't cut herself. Nine times out of ten, I didn't have to ask for an instrument, I'd just look up, and she had it ready. She *anticipated* my needs, you see. She followed the surgery as it developed, she knew what came next, she knew what complications might arise, and she was ready for all of it."

"Sounds like a huge loss for your department," said Bobby.

"Oh, it is, but that doesn't stack up against the loss of her life."

"No, of course not," said Meredeth. "What do you know about Mary Ann, the person?"

"Well, as I said, I didn't know her socially."

"Doctors and nurses don't mix?" asked Cliff. "That seems strange given how many doctors marry their nurses."

Gull chuckled. "Yes, that does go on. Mary Ann wasn't..." He shook his head. "I don't want to speak ill of the dead, so let's leave it that Mary Ann wasn't my type outside of the OR."

"No?" asked Meredeth, arching one eyebrow.

"No," said Gull with a shake of the head for emphasis.

"What made her not your type?" asked Cliff. "Did she like classic rock and you're more of a dubstep kind of guy?"

Gull shot a perplexed look his way. "I'm reserved in my personal life. I don't like being the center of attention—I get enough of that in the OR. Mary Ann...well, let it suffice that she thought differently."

"And that's all?" asked Roger, one eyebrow arched. "She wanted attention?"

"No," said Gull. "She was loud, she drew attention to herself and whoever she was with She was more interested in *right now* than the future if you take my meaning."

"And how do you know this if you never socialized with her?" asked Bobby.

"We happened to enjoy some of the same clubs. I wasn't *with* her and Liz, but I did have several opportunities to observe their behavior in social situations."

"Ah, I see."

Meredeth leaned forward in her chair. "Tell me, Dr. Gull, on those occasions when you saw Liz and Mary Ann at a nightclub, did you notice anyone watching them from afar? Or maybe surreptitiously?"

"A lot of men watched Mary Ann. I came to believe it was what she wanted."

"Anyone, in particular, raise the hair on the back of your neck?" asked Bobby. "Anyone seem overly interested?"

Gull frowned and looked down at his blotter. "I'll have to give that some thought. It wasn't like I was alone or just sat there staring at them. I was there with someone—a date, you understand—and only spared a glance now and then at my nurses."

"Okay," said Meredeth, taking out a business card and sliding it onto his blotter. "Please give me a call if you remember anyone."

"Of course," said Dr. Gull. "But please understand that those dance clubs are full of people. I *will* scour my memory for someone who stands out, but my understanding is that most serial killers are adept at blending in."

"Don't believe everything you see or read on the subject," said Meredeth.

"You mean that's not true?"

"No, it is true for some serial killers, but not every single one, or even most."

Dr. Gull turned forty-five degrees so he could cross his long legs. "Ah. You seem to know who I meant when I said 'Liz.'"

"We spoke to Elizabeth Pacer a few minutes ago. She told us she and Mary Ann went to those clubs."

"Yes, I see."

"If we can turn back to Kindred Haven, I understand that Mary Ann was held up to the staff as someone to emulate, and that didn't sit well with everyone."

"The ones I forced to return to a level of care that was more suitable to their personalities, I assume?"

Meredeth nodded. "Did anyone make threats? Did anyone direct their anger at Mary Ann?"

Gull shook his head. "I don't believe your unsub is a hospital employee." He steepled his fingers in front of his face once more. "Taking a life is antithetical to what we do here, to our mindsets."

"That may be true in most cases, but perhaps not all," Bobby said.

Again, Meredeth caught a flash of annoyance on Dr. Gull's face and wondered at it. Was it just his annoyance at being contradicted—something she didn't imagine he allowed in his professional life—or something else? "You may be correct, Dr. Gull, but it's procedure to eliminate those people in the victim's personal life, including co-workers. It's clear from the staging of the crime that this wasn't supposed to look like a personal crime—not an ex-boyfriend or anything like that—but oftentimes, a serial killer may get a job at the same place as his would-be victim in order to have an easier time tracking her movements, her habits, her schedule."

"I see. Then someone not on the medical staff. HR or administration or janitorial?"

"That could very well be true, but we must also consider that this might actually be a personal crime disguised as a serial act, after all."

"You mean someone may have pretended to be a serial killer to throw the police off track?"

"Exactly. Now, circling back to those disgruntled nurses, do any of them have spouses who might have taken things personally? Anyone who might, themselves, have considered revenge justified?"

"No, not the nurses, but a spouse?" He shrugged. "I'm afraid I have no idea."

"No one threatened you? No one called to discuss the move with you?"

Dr. Gull shook his head and glanced at the clock.

"Are we keeping you?" asked Cliff.

"No, not yet. I do have a surgery in ten minutes' time, however, so we will need to end soon."

Meredeth leaned forward and tapped her business card. "Please give it some thought and reach out to me."

"I will, I assure you."

"In that case, if no one else has any follow-ups..." She turned and looked at Bobby, then Roger and Cliff. When no one spoke up, she stood. "Thank you for taking the time out of your busy schedule to speak with us, Dr. Gull. May we reach out if we run into something we can't explain?"

"Of course. I'm happy to help in any context, including medical. For instance, I'm willing to assist if your ME isn't quite up to par."

"Thank you," Meredeth said, then turned and led Bobby, Cliff, and Roger out of the room.

CHAPTER 13

WINDOW SHOPPING

Sherman Oaks, CA

MICHAEL WATCHED CONNELLY in the reflection of the hospital's glass front, followed by her damn Marine guard dog. She paused to stand in the sun a moment, head back, eyes closed. *Enjoy the sunshine*, he thought. *Enjoy it while I allow you the chance.* Fury bubbled within, fury at the intrusion into his hunting ground, fury at the questions she was asking everyone, fury at those who deigned to *help* her.

Meredeth pointed across the street, and at first, he thought she was pointing at the Italian bar and grill with the ridiculous name and hoped to God she wasn't thinking of lunch there. He followed along, his head turned toward the glass displays, watching her, watching Connelly, and dreaming dark dreams.

My plans are ruined! he raged. *I had a timeline! I had a schedule!* But all that was blown by Connelly's appearance. He'd have to re-evaluate his plans, advance his timeline, push his schedule—that meant he might need to improvise, and he didn't want to do that. He wanted everything to be perfect. He wanted to wait, to drop his next victim eight nights in the future. He wanted to wait until the time was right, but with Connelly on the scene, he didn't dare. He'd have to rush, maybe even change the order of his planned victims, perhaps even taking someone at random. Frustration bubbled within, but he kept his face still, aloof. Feigning distraction in case someone decided to speak to him.

Without pausing, Connelly turned away from Ventura, turning down the alley—*his* alley— without a word, without a signal. *At least she hadn't suggested they eat at the Trattoria Del Sole*, he thought. Her crew also walked in silence, though the jarhead was smiling as if he'd shared a joke with the LASD idiot beside him.

Michael couldn't wait to go home, to sit alone in the cold darkness and just think. To think his way out of the predicament he felt closing in around him.

Then again, maybe he should just take a vacation. Perhaps he should put his plans on hold and just go. The trail would get cold, and the FBI would recall Connelly and the grunt. When it was all safe again, he could pick up where he'd left off. Maybe, if he were extremely lucky, he could even keep his old schedule.

Or he could take a vacation somewhere and pick a replacement for the woman he'd watched for months, then decided she'd make a good victim number two. He could pull someone at random—his desire to only kill sluts and whores was strong, but so was his lust for freedom.

He needed time to *think*. Time when he wasn't distracted by trying to trail Connelly and her crew of lap dogs. He needed to do what he could to get away and go home. He always thought better in the dark.

And that made sense, given his black desires.

CHAPTER 14

IN DARKNESS

David Branch's Farm, NY

THEY SAT STILL, Carl and Michelina. The naked flesh of her hip rested against his own, and it was a distraction, but he felt the need to think, to sit silently and run everything through the old hopper. Michelina was a nice girl, and she'd taken him to a height that Lucy never had before her orgasm and his slammed through them both. He wanted to try it again, but...

Thoughts of Lucy, of what she was, what she'd used him to accomplish, refused to lie still. She'd never allowed him to sit in silence after, always consumed by a bouncing happiness and the need to run her mouth. She was young—though not that much younger than he, only three years—and he supposed that was a major difference between her and Michelina, but it wasn't the only one.

Lucy was a girl—he could even picture her in high school somewhere, chasing football players and converting them to worshippers of the ground she walked on. She'd never have taken up cheerleading or anything mundane like that, but she'd have made sure she was prettier than them all—or sluttier.

Michelina ran her hand up his spine and ran her fingers through his dark hair. "I enjoyed that," she murmured.

"Enjoyed is too weak a word."

She laughed, a chiming sound that ran through the woods around them. "Your thoughts were heavy, dark."

It wasn't a question, but he felt compelled to answer as if it were. "Yes. Lucy."

"Oh," said Michelina softly.

"Don't worry. My thoughts in that regard are angry, cold."

"I'm not worried, Carl. I'll take what I can get."

"Good, because I plan on keeping you busy for a while tonight."

She ran a finger down the edge of his ear. "Just tonight?"

"For a start."

"Then what are we waiting for? Or do you want to go on thinking about that little tramp? Because if you do, that's cool. I'll sit here while you finish your dark dreams until you're ready to give me all your attention."

Chuckling, Carl turned to face her. "You ready again, already?"

"Girls don't need time to get ready again, Carl. The right girl is always ready for her guy."

"What about Mack?"

"Mack's not here, is he?"

Grinning, Carl leaned toward her and brushed his lips against hers. "No," he said without withdrawing his head. "But I am."

"Bingo," she said in a husky breath.

CHAPTER 15

HANGRY

Sherman Oaks, CA

THEY REACHED THE Impala without seeing another soul in the alleyway, and once again, Meredeth's gaze was magnetized to the crime scene. She stood near the rear passenger door, her back to it, facing the alley, her gaze zipping from point to point. She noted the difference in the shadows in the late afternoon light and tried to imagine the scene in moonlight or no light. "I'd like to come back when it's dark," she said.

"We can do that," said Cliff. "How about we find a nice sit-down place and have dinner? We'd beat the rush if we went now, and we can relax a bit. Rest up."

"That sounds like a perfect plan," said Bobby.

"Sure." Meredeth didn't make a move to enter the car, however. "How long until full dark?"

"Sunset's around half past six," said Roger. Like Meredeth, his gaze was fixed on the scene, but in his case, he stared at the spot where Mary Ann's body had lain.

"And that's only an hour and fifteen minutes from now," said Cliff. "But it won't be very dark until later. Say eight o'clock."

"So maybe we have a leisurely dinner, then go and check in—unless it's too far away—and come back?"

Cliff nodded at Bobby across the roof of the car. "That sounds reasonable. What do you two like to eat?"

"Anything," said Meredeth. "We're not picky."

"Speak for yourself," said Bobby. "Does Sherman Oaks have good barbeque?"

"As a matter of fact, the best place in L.A. is only a couple of blocks down Ventura."

"Excellent," said Bobby.

"The bone place?" asked Roger, his mouth pulled down into a frown.

"Not a big fan?" asked Meredeth. Roger glanced at her but then returned his attention to Cliff.

"Yes, Boneyard Bistro. It's consistently given the highest marks."

"Sounds great," said Bobby, "as long as it isn't some frou-frou West Coast barbeque sauce."

Roger shifted from foot to foot, his gaze drawn to the spot where Blocker bled out. "I hate barbeque," he muttered.

"Don't mind him," said Cliff. "You can have a burger, Rog. And to answer Van Zandt's question, they do Santa Maria-style barbeque, but also Texas, North Carolina, and

St. Louis-style rubs. They really have something for everyone."

"Mere?" asked Bobby.

"Sounds good to me. Let's make a move."

Roger pulled his gaze away from the scene and glowered at Cliff for a moment. "I think I'll pass on dinner." He tossed the keys to Cliff, then turned and walked back toward Ventura.

"We can do something else," called Bobby, but Roger only lifted his hand and waved it back and forth without breaking his stride.

"Don't mind Roger," said Cliff. "He gets hangry this time of day."

"Well, now I feel bad."

"Don't, Bobby. He's just that way. And, truth to tell, he's a bit of a lone wolf. He can only stand so much 'people time,' as he calls it. He'll be back to his normal level of grump in the morning."

"But—"

"Trust me. This is just who Roger is. He probably wouldn't have come along no matter what restaurant we chose." Cliff circled around the front of the car. "One of you want to switch to the front?"

"You take shotgun, Bobby," said Meredeth.

Cliff unlocked the unmarked cruiser, and they all piled in. He backed them into the alley proper and pointed the car at Ventura. By the time they reached it, Roger was already two blocks away and walking fast, his head down.

"I thought he was going to get an uber."

"He will. Eventually," said Cliff. "He probably didn't want to risk having to talk to us again. Don't worry. He's fine."

"If you say so," she said, her gaze following the tall, dark-haired detective as he walked away, never once glancing back. She found his behavior a bit odd—or maybe his choice of profession. *Why would anyone who dislikes dealing with people pick law enforcement? Why subject himself to constantly feeling uncomfortable and wanting to get away?*

Cliff turned right. "Boneyard is only a dozen blocks or so. I hope you brought your appetites. We'll be there in fifteen minutes or so."

Meredeth was familiar with D.C. traffic, so she didn't bat an eye at the block-per-minute time projection. She turned and glanced out the back window, expecting to see Roger walking toward the upcoming sunset, but instead, he'd crossed to the other side of the road and stood staring after them. His face was flat as if carved from stone, and in some deep corner of Meredeth's mind, an alarm buzzer rang. "How long have you and Roger partnered up?"

Cliff glanced at her in the rearview mirror. "About six years, I think. He's always been this way. You don't know how many times I've invited him to dinner and had him walk away like this." He shrugged a shoulder and turned his eyes back to the road. "He's also a picky eater. *And* he's on a health kick at the moment."

"I see," she said, taking one more look behind them. But this time, Roger was nowhere in sight.

CHAPTER 16

LIGHTS OUT

Sherman Oaks, CA

HER "UPGRADED" ROOM didn't appear very different from the regular rooms despite the "suite" label. It was the same size as a regular room, but instead of the bathroom being close to the door, it had been moved to the approximate middle of the room, opening onto a short hall that connected the "bedroom"—a bed, an older model television, and a closet—with the "living room"—a couch, a two-year-old TV, and a round table with three chairs shoved up under the television. There was a standard hotel safe in the closet in case she needed to leave valuables in the room, but hers only blinked its lights when she tried to set the combination.

She had her ice bucket filled and a couple of cans of coke chilling in the ice, just in case. But besides a few minor stabs, her head didn't feel that bad. Then again, it was only the beginning of the case, and she felt sure there would be more bodies, more victims, more bloody murder scenes coming along sooner rather than later.

Her phone pressed against her ear, she propped a couple of pillows against the headboard, then plopped on the bed, sitting up straight, with her legs crossed before her. The phone rang four times before Kevin's voicemail kicked in, and she sighed while his greeting ran down. "I'd like to report an emergency," she said after the beep. "I've got a fire that needs putting out. If you think you can help, give me a call back." She clicked off and dropped the phone next to her on the bed. It was nine o'clock in Sherman Oaks, which made it midnight back in Virginia, but she remembered enough of her own time as a cadet to know no one was sleeping yet.

She glanced at the remote for the TV, but honestly, she had no idea what she'd watch even if she did turn the boob tube on. She'd spent too much time watching mindless television while recovering from Alex's best attempt to kill her. She had little desire to add to those memories, so she moved the remote from the bed into the nightstand's drawer.

With a sigh, she snuggled down under the bedclothes, then reached up and killed the lamp on the nightstand. She picked up her phone to check that her alarm was set and turned on and was moving the phone to the nightstand when it rang. She smiled at the caller ID and accepted the call. "Hello? Is this the fire department?"

"If only I was within driving distance," Kevin said with a chuckle. "How's Hollywood?"

"I don't know. We're in Sherman Oaks."

"Have you seen Tom Cruise yet?"

"No, but then again, he's so short I might have overlooked him."

"Har, har," said Kevin. "How's Bobby? Are the locals cooperative?"

"He's fine, and the local detectives are happy we're here. At least one of them."

"Ah. They just don't know you yet."

"Who? The one who's happy we're here?"

"Well, I won't rule out that possibility, but I meant the one who isn't. What's his malfunction?"

"I don't know. I don't even know if he really is malfunctioning." She told him the story about choosing a restaurant for dinner, including how Cliff had defended the man. "But the most unsettling part is what he did after he left. He walked in the opposite direction on Ventura, but after we'd pulled out, I turned around, and he was staring at us and across the street. I turned to speak to Cliff, and then when I looked back, Roger was gone."

"And your suspicious nature has taken over."

"Well, isn't his behavior strange?"

"Strange? Yes. Criminal? No."

"You only make that distinction because you're in overt threat mode. Typical SWAT mentality."

Kevin chuckled and said, "Typical profiler mentality on your part. But I've got to be honest with you, I called with my fire helmet on."

"Oh? And what else?"

"Suspenders—though with nothing to attach them to seem a little silly."

It was Meredeth's turn to laugh.

"And you, FBI? What are you wearing while this fire burns inside you?"

"Guess."

"Hmm. This is a tough one. Ratty old men's T-shirt that hides every one of your beautiful curves?"

"I think I could grow to like you, Saunders."

"Think so?"

"Yeah. You say all the right things."

"I pride myself on that ability. Here's another example: our cell phones have video capabilities."

"I like the way you think."

"I like the way you...well, everything."

"There you go again with the right things to say, but not yet."

"No? Should I take off the suspenders?"

"Definitely. Tell me about the rest of your day."

"Boring. Classes, the Yellow Brick Road, more shooting."

"Oh, if you're too tired..." She grinned, knowing what he'd say.

"Oh, no. I feel like I just woke up from twelve hours of uninterrupted rest."

"How did I know you'd say that?"

"Because you are as brilliant as you are beautiful?"

"Good answer but keep the heat down for a few minutes more and you'll get what you want."

"Promise?"

"Hey, I called you, remember? Fire, etc.?"

"Then talk me through your case. And, FBI?"

"Yes?"

"Talk fast."

She laughed aloud, then spoke through her smile. "The case is going to get intense; I can feel it in my bones. We interviewed some of the victim's co-workers, and they painted a picture of a good employee, a good colleague, but socially, she was wild."

"Maybe she had a fire within, too."

She chuckled low in her throat. "Maybe she did. But she tried to put it out with a varied diet."

"Ah. One-night stands?"

"That was the impression I got. Not that her murder is her own fault or anything."

"Of course not. It only makes the suspect pool pretty wide."

"Yep. Her boss is a strange one. Dr. Aaron Gull, Chief of Surgery."

"Beyond the name, how is he strange?"

"There's nothing I can put my finger on, but there's definitely *something*. He went to great lengths to emphasize how he didn't know Blocker socially, but then he later admitted he went to the same clubs where she was picking up her dates. Of course, he was there with another woman, and not at all interested in Mary Ann."

"Oh, of course. He wasn't staring at all, was he?"

"Not the way he tells it. According to him, he just glanced over from time to time, but he knew a lot of details about Liz and Mary Ann's nights out."

"Liz?"

"Elizabeth Pacer, RN. Friend and co-worker."

"Ah."

"So Gull's got a crush on his underlings. What else sets him apart?"

"His behavior just struck me as...insincere."

"Liar?"

"I don't know that, but he's hiding something, I think. He may have had a fling with the victim."

"Hopefully, *before* she was killed."

"Ew!"

"I'm just saying what you're thinking, Mere."

"I'm a good girl, Saunders. I don't think about necrophilia." She took a breath and let it out slowly. "Anyway, I'm going to look into his past, see where he worked last, where he went to school, etc."

"That sounds warranted," said Kevin in a solemn tone. "He might just be a dirty old man, though, so don't set that brilliant mind of yours on him."

"I won't unless the evidence warrants it."

"I know, Mere. Tell me about the scene."

"At first glance, it seems like the perfect place to stage a murder, but there aren't many places to hide, and I'm sure he attacked in ambush."

"No place to hide or no *good* places?"

"There are some juvenile trees on one side, but the other side is two-car garages with shrubs at each wall separating them. I suppose he could have pressed himself into the corner of the garage doors and the side wall."

"And used the shrubs for cover."

"Yeah. It wouldn't be perfect, and in the daylight, he'd have been spotted instantly, but we went back after dark, and without a flashlight, the shadows would have kept him hidden until she was almost on top of him."

"Luck or planning?"

"I'd guess planning. He's an organized killer, but he's pretending he's not. Plus, he probably broke all the lights."

Kevin was silent a moment, drinking that in. "Pretending?"

"Yeah. He's pretending he's Jack the Ripper reincarnated, but he can't hide his nature. He brought a heavy-bladed knife—Jack used a Liston amputation knife set. We'll see the ME and the victim's corpse tomorrow, but I'm betting the unsub also used a Liston, or something very like it. Also, he painted the first couple of lines from a poem featured in one of the more disputed Jack the Ripper letters on the wall, but he wasn't exact."

"The 'little whores' poem?"

"Yes, but he wrote, 'Eight little whores. No hope of heaven.'"

"What's the original quote?"

"'Eight little whores, with no hope of heaven.'"

"I don't know, Mere. That's pretty close."

"It is, but an organized copycat would be *exact*. Everything would have to match the original crime."

"Maybe he was rushed. Or maybe caught up in the killing part."

"Yes, both are possibilities, but I'll tell you, Kev, I get the feeling he did it on purpose. I think he's trying to throw off the profile."

"That's a difficult thing to accomplish. Especially with you on the case."

"That part is easy. I bet he didn't expect us to show up until the third body hit the pavement. At the very earliest. He thought he'd only be facing the LASD Homicide Division, and he wanted to paint them a picture of someone else."

"And from the sounds of it, he may be one of the LASD detectives."

"What? You mean Roger?" she asked.

"Didn't you say he's setting off alarm bells? Didn't Alex do the same thing when you thought he was Sonya Sargent?"

"Well, yes, but—"

"And didn't Michelina say at least one of Ankou's victims was in law enforcement?"

"Yes, she did, but I'm not in the habit of accusing fellow officers."

"No, that duty falls to Van Zandt, doesn't it?"

"Kevin, I didn't mean—"

"I know. And you told me you didn't believe Bobby when he suspected me, that you kept trying to chill him out, but after what happened in St. Pete, I think you need to give him free rein. And I think you need to stop dismissing your instincts—after all, you've spent twenty-some-odd years developing them. Give Michelina a call and ask her about this Roger character."

"Maybe you're right, Kev."

"I am. I'm also right about switching this call to video before you fall asleep."

"Ah ha," she said and pressed the button to switch over.

CHAPTER 17
THEN THERE ARE FIVE
Sherman Oaks, CA

MICHAEL DRUITT LOUNGED against the bar, playing the relaxed drinker, his back against the polished oak, a beer bottle in one hand, the other hanging limp from the bar, one foot on the brass rest. The dance floor looked like a multi-headed, multi-limbed creature of destruction, couples bouncing, leaping, flagging their arms overhead, a hydra of sex, drugs, and rock and roll. He fancied he could smell the lust, the pheromones, the musk of attraction, and his nostrils flared with each indrawn breath.

She was out there, dancing with a different man every song as if trying them on and discarding them as blemished goods. She was a beauty, he couldn't argue that she wasn't, and it seemed like every man in the club wanted a piece of her. He grinned at that thought, a secret little grin, full of surreptitious knowledge, precognition of how her night would end.

His backpack lay between his feet and the bar, and in it his Liston knife set—three blades strong enough for amputation—and his other toys sat hidden and safe. He spent a few minutes pretending she was the FBI agent who plagued his fantasies—one Meredeth Connelly by name. He shook his head, knowing Connelly wasn't on the menu, at least not yet, but he couldn't help fantasizing about how he would take her life when the countdown ended.

It was approaching closing time, and he found it harder and harder to wait, to stand still and watch without being too obvious. Some men enjoyed the so-called gentlemen's clubs with all that gyrating flesh sans clothing, but Michael found his current pursuit much more exciting. Yes, he planned on seeing the woman he was watching naked, but not while she was still alive. They had business, she and he.

When the bartender announced last call, she strode off the dance floor, ignoring the calls, the outstretched hands, and walked to the bar. She sidled up to the only open bit of real estate—which happened to be right next to Michael.

He swigged his beer while she ordered, then glanced to the side to find her looking at him, a small smile playing at the corners of her mouth. "You like watching," she said.

He nodded once. "I do...when there's someone worth watching."

Her cheeks pinked up a little, and she smiled. "But you don't like dancing?"

"Not the kind where you have to stand up."

"Oh, la, la," she said with a laugh. "I thought you were shy and sexy. Now I know you are just sexy."

"Thanks. I don't think I should tell you what I think about you."

Her smile widened. "Words are cheap, bucko. Why don't we go somewhere, and you can *show* me what you think of me."

He dropped his gaze down to her Louboutin FMPs, then let his gaze crawl upward slowly, drinking her in, and his nostrils flared to take in her scent—the sweat, the musk of her sex, the dregs of her perfume. His gaze slowed below her waist, then traced upward over her belly button and paused again at her breasts. When his eyes finally reached her eyes, he hit her with his most charming smile. "That would be my pleasure."

She laughed and lay her hand on his arm. "I take it you like what you see."

"Nah, I *love* what I see. It might scare you if I were to tell you the things I plan on doing to you."

Another laugh. "I don't scare easily, Mister..." She quirked her eyebrow at him.

"Call me Ken. Ken Reynolds."

"That's a good name. If you can make good on your veiled promises, I'll scream it while you ravish me."

"It's a date," he said and turned to face her, still leaning against the bar on his elbow.

She lifted her drink, never taking her eyes off his, and drank it down. "Finish your beer, cowboy."

He grinned and drained the water out of his beer bottle, then slid it across the bar and held out his hand to her. She slid her palm into his and winked as she pulled him toward the door. He let her lead—it was clear she had a quiet place in mind, maybe her apartment, maybe in a park somewhere, but either way, he'd watch for his opportunity to pull her into a dark alley and have his way.

The night air was cool—a relief from the stuffy confines of the nightclub. She continued leading him away from the club, from the crowds, smiling, eyes twinkling. "My name is Molly," she said.

"I think I'll call you Annie, instead."

Her laugh rolled out and echoed down the street. "Okay. As long as you scream it when the time comes."

"Oh, don't worry on that account." He grinned at her, and for a moment, she hesitated, her brows caught somewhere between bunched up with worry and an inquisitive arch. "I'll tell the world about you, my darling," he said and lifted her hand to brush his lips.

Molly cocked her head to the side a moment, then laughed aloud. "I can't figure you out, Ken. I can't decide if you're really weird or just different from every man who only wants to get in my panties."

"A bit of both, most likely," he said with a grin. His gaze darted over her shoulder.

She turned to follow his gaze into the pitch-black concrete channel of the Los Angeles River that bisected Sherman Oaks. "Kinky," she said in a breathy voice. "But I don't want to get wet. At least not on the outside." She tittered and pulled him toward the ramp that descended through the trees and eventually came out on the concrete riverbed. "Do you think anyone will see us?"

"Not in time to stop me from ravishing you," he said with a secret smile.

Once more, she cocked her head, but this time she squinted a little as she regarded him. "Should I get all the way naked?"

He squeezed her hand. "Let me take care of that." He took the lead, walking quickly down the ramp, unslinging his backpack as he went.

"My, my," she said in a voice that dripped lust. "You're an eager soul, aren't you?"

"My dear, you have no idea how long I've denied myself, how long I've planned this night."

She raised an eyebrow. "Are you stalking me?"

"Such a strange word, stalking. So many implications, both bad and good. But to answer you, in a way I have stalked you. You're very hard to miss out on the dance floor. I've been watching...dreaming of tonight."

The white of the moonlight reflecting on her teeth flashed a moment, then her lips were on his.

It was almost too easy, but it did underscore the appropriateness of his choice. She was a slut, and very soon, she'd pay for it.

CHAPTER 18

CALLED OUT

Sherman Oaks, CA

WHEN MEREDETH OPENED the car door, the feeling of being watched by something big, fierce, and hungry washed over her. She remained calm as it was a feeling she was familiar with, something she trained for, and something she called "getting the hinkies." She climbed out of the car and looked around, her gaze zipping from shadowed doorway to dark roof to stygian landscaping. She didn't put her hand on her pistol butt, no matter how much better it might make her feel. She was intimately aware that their unsub might be watching—no, *probably was* watching. It went with the territory. Even so, that feeling of receiving an apex predator's full attention lingered, sending chills racing up and down her spine, and she eyed the dark trees surrounding the path to the ramp that led down to the L.A. River.

She glanced at Bobby, an assessing gaze, and decided he felt it, too. Bobby's danger sense was even more refined than her own. She had years on him as an FBI Agent, but his experiences as a member of the Marine Corps Force Recon gave him the absolute edge in close quarters combat as well as the ability to make snap evaluations of potentially deadly situations. He glanced at her and smiled.

He feels it, but the danger is remote, she thought. She nodded back, then turned to Cliff and took him by the arm. "Chances are high that the unsub is concealed nearby, watching us."

Cliff nodded and visibly restrained himself from looking around.

"Where's your partner?" she asked, smiling as if nothing were amiss.

"I couldn't raise him. My calls went straight to voice mail, and my texts have gone unread. I sent an officer by his place."

"I see." She dropped her hand from his elbow and turned toward the sea of flashing red and blue lights. She set off toward the yellow tape which set off "normal" pavement from the pavement that might contain evidence, blood or otherwise. An LA County Deputy stood nearby, logging everyone who entered or exited the scene. She walked up to him and presented her ID wallet, then turned to Cliff, who had followed her. "I'd like to walk the scene."

"Of course," he said.

She continued to look at him.

"Oh! Right, give me a second." He nodded to the deputy and signed the log, then ducked under the tape.

Bobby came up beside her and gave the deputy his credentials, then turned to Meredeth. "I'm going to walk the perimeter."

"Wait for McCloe," she said.

He jerked his chin to the side. "I'd rather go alone. I don't know what his capabilities are."

"You need backup."

"No, I don't."

"Yes, you do. You and Cliff can walk the perimeter—maybe tell him to go ahead of you if he's hopeless but keep him in sight at all times while you do your ninja act. His safety is your responsibility."

"It might be hard to babysit and track the unsub."

"You can handle it, Marine. I'll walk the scene, then wait for you two to get back. This is a fresh scene, Bobby. I want to see it before anyone changes anything."

"I know, Mere. I'll take Cliff with me."

The deputy followed their conversation wide-eyed, bouncing his gaze back and forth between them like they were tennis players at the U.S. Open. When Meredeth caught his eye and smiled, he blushed red to the roots of his close-cropped brown hair.

Cliff came jogging back, his hair flying in the wind. "You're on, Connelly," he called from twenty feet away.

"You're with me, Cliff," said Bobby. "Tell me you have some tactical training."

"In my youth. Army."

"Marines," grunted Bobby. "Force Recon. I want you ahead of me while we walk the perimeter. I'll have your back, even if you lose track of me. If I yell, drop on your face, and I mean *right now*."

"Ten-four," said Cliff. "You think he's still here?"

"Absolutely," said Meredeth, eyeing the rooftops again. "Bobby, remember all three dimensions."

"Come on, McCloe, let's get invisible." The two men turned and jogged back to where they'd parked near the corner of Valleyheart Drive and Coldwater Canyon Avenue.

Meredeth watched them for a moment, knowing they'd be exposed when they crossed over the river on Coldwater Canyon. She turned and ducked under the yellow tape. It was up to her to draw and keep the unsub's attention if she could. She jogged down to where the path turned one hundred and eighty degrees and became a ramp. She drew her compact Maglite from her back pocket and looked down at it as if testing the light, but really showing off her face to anyone looking. She wanted the unsub to see her, to latch his gaze on her.

Even though the LASD had vacated the scene without an argument, she called, "Hey, you! Yes, you, Detective! You're supposed to be out of here!" She strode down the ramp like a woman consumed with self-importance and ire. Her pulse pounded at the idea of descending into that blackness at the bottom of the ramp, especially knowing she was all alone and that Bobby *wasn't* on overwatch, but she went anyway, her head held high, her back laser straight. She flashed her light back and forth in front of her, making a bullet magnet of herself, and, truth be told, not looking where the bright disc of light landed but watching the shadows across the concrete bed of the river.

She reached the bottom of the ramp and clicked off the light for a moment, reoriented it, and clicked it back on, suddenly illuminating the far bank of the river and the walking path at its top. There was no one there, and she felt foolish. She dropped the beam of the light to the ground in front of her and stepped around the remains of the L.A. River, avoiding getting her field boots soaking wet. She proceeded under the Coldwater Canyon overpass and stopped, her Maglite lighting up the cave-like river channel.

A deceased woman lay on her back in the dead center of the velvet shadows cast by the overpass overhead. Her legs were bent at the knees, and her feet were flat on the ground. Her dress lay in a pile next to the southern bank. Her left arm was flung across her left breast, and her right arm was splayed northward as if reaching for something.

The rank smell of stagnant water battled with the smell of the eviscerated decedent. Her small intestines lay in a pile on and above her right shoulder, a rivulet of blood trailing down into the standing water. Her intestines were still attached, a thick, ropey strand of intestine snaking from the pile above her shoulder across her right breast and into her opened abdomen. The unsub had taken two flaps of skin and flesh from her lower abdomen and splattered them above her left shoulder where they had deposited a large quantity of blood on the concrete. Her savaged throat was partially hidden by a handkerchief, which was now soaked in blood. Her face was swollen and turned to the right, and her swollen tongue extended through her teeth but didn't break the plane of her lips.

In other words, almost exactly like the second Jack the Ripper scene.

CHAPTER 19

CAT AND MOUSE

Sherman Oaks, CA

BOBBY WATCHED CLIFF moving ahead of him down the north side of the dark and sleepy Valleyheart Drive North. He was on the opposite side of the road, setup in the doorway of the narrow commercial building on the corner of Valleyheart and Coldwater Canyon. The doorway he crouched in was the last bit of cover on the south side of the street until he got past the tiny parking area and could hide in the foliage a hundred yards ahead.

The night was quiet on this side of the river, and he could hear Cliff huffing with the stress and excitement. He was almost past the point where Bobby would again find cover, almost to the Infiniti Q45 parked in the street directly under a no-parking sign.

Bobby had his pistol out, a round chambered and ready. His finger was indexed on the polymer frame of his Glock, but he knew from thousands of hours of training that he could rectify that in a New York second. He wished for a red dot, as he always did in situations like the one he found himself in, or better yet, for an M4 like he'd carried into battle, though the carbine would be harder to conceal under his coat.

Cliff pulled up behind the Infiniti, holding his own pistol in a two-handed grip that looked marginally competent, and glanced back at Van Zandt. Bobby nodded, then hunched his back and sprinted across the road into the driveway of the multi-family building there. He squatted behind the hedge that hid the rest of Valleyheart from view, controlling his breathing for a moment before rounding the corner and sprinting for the four-foot concrete block wall to the right of the SUV. Cliff had his gun on the Q45's roof, pointing down range, ready to offer suppressing fire if the need arose.

Bobby ran across the road and into the concealing shrubs and trees. He crouched, steadying his pistol by resting the flesh of his left forearm against the trunk of a tree. He drew breath in through his mouth and exhaled through his nose, watching for movement, for a silhouette against the night sky or streetlights.

Cliff moved up, taking cover in the overgrown landscaping at the next house. He glanced back at the point where Bobby had disappeared into the bushes, then peered around trying to catch sight of him. Bobby moved deliberately forward, careful to avoid noise, trying to keep close to abreast of Cliff's position as he advanced. The feeling of being watched continued to set his nerves thrumming, and he wished for a nice night-vision rig.

Nothing moved on the street ahead of them, and Bobby paused to scan behind them, checking the rooftops of the apartments and multi-family homes back toward the intersection. He also took a look at that narrow commercial building but had no joy on any of them. He wondered if the unsub might be *inside* that commercial building, maybe watching them with night vision of his own, shielded from view by the reflective window coating that treated all the windows of the building.

He whistled, long and low, and hoped Cliff got the message. He turned and duckwalked back the way he'd come, the feeling of being watched getting stronger as he did so. He stopped at the edge of the foliage, then opened his eyes wide for a four-count, blinked, opened them wide again, then repeated the process twice more. It was a technique he'd learned from a Navy SEAL for improving not only night vision but visual acuity.

He stared at the building for perhaps five minutes without moving, barely even breathing, but nothing inside was visible, no matter how many times he did the eye-widening trick. A giant billboard loomed over the building, with catwalks on either side. Bobby peered up at it, focusing on an anomalous black lump—like that of a prone man, though it seemed too small for a human. Even so, he stared at it, watching for movement, for breathing, for the glint of an optic.

And that's when he saw movement on the roof of the building across Coldwater Canyon Avenue.

CHAPTER 20

CALLED OUT, AGAIN

Sherman Oaks, CA

MEREDETH SQUATTED AND pulled on a pair of gloves, laying her Maglite on the ground so that it shined on the victim. Her throat had suffered a long gash that nearly encircled the woman's throat, and if Meredeth's guess was correct, it ran from the victim's left to her right, just the way Jack the Ripper had sliced Dark Annie's throat back in 1888. She glanced at the crater that existed where the woman's belly had once been. Again, she assumed that the wound would match Dark Annie's—and that some of her organs would be missing from the area, including her womb, bladder, and part of her vagina.

She rolled her Maglite so that it focused on the decedent's face, noting the bruise over her right temple, two thumb-like bruises on her upper chest, a bruise on her right cheek, and three meticulously placed scratches a couple of inches below her left jaw, going in the opposite direction from the throat cut.

"I'm sorry," she murmured to the corpse. "I'm sorry I was too late to save you, but I'll get the bastard that did this to you." She pulled off her gloves, turning them inside-out in the process, and shoved them into her back pocket. She grabbed her little Maglite and turned, then froze.

The unsub had once again fingerpainted a few lines of poetry on the wall. They read:

> Connelly might save one, then there'll be seven.
> Seven little whores, all far too willing.
> This one stays here, there's been a killing.
>
> Catch me if you can, Connelly.

Meredeth grimaced and drew a breath deep into her lungs, her nostrils flaring, drinking in the stink of the riverbed, of blood, of the woman's last corporeal acts. He'd broken the pattern; he'd intentionally misquoted the verse—customized it to fit the present moment rather than duplicating the original verse, which may or may not have been written by Jack the Ripper himself.

She didn't like what the changes implied. She didn't like the accelerated pace, and she didn't like having the poem include her name, nor the direct call-out in the last line. She turned and glanced back at the victim, guessing her name would not be Annie. She shook her head, cursing her fame and the fact it meant this woman's death.

She sighed and turned her attention to the concrete beneath her feet, sweeping her Maglite back and forth across its rough surface, looking for and finding both the scuff marks from the woman's shoes and the black skid marks from the unsubs rubber-soled boots. She followed the marks to where the scuffle had started, then turned back and examined the scene again, looking at the woman's Louboutin's and shaking her head.

She heaved a sigh, then turned and slowly climbed the ramp back to street level, sweeping her light from left to right, then from right to left, searching for any cast-off trinket but finding nothing. It was then that she noticed the feeling of being stalked by an apex hunter was gone.

She reached the top of the ramp and turned back toward the street corner, clicking off her Maglite and slipping it back into her pocket. Her mind was awhirl with thoughts, with plans, with strategies for bringing the nocturnal asshole out into the light. *Maybe I should do a press conference*, she thought. *Or I could give an interview like I gave Goode. Or perhaps—*

Her phone buzzed in her pocket, and she drew it out and glanced at the screen. It was a text from Bobby that read:

> *10-66, corner of Valleyheart N and Coldwater. East side, roof.*

Meredeth sprinted toward the C3 and the group of officers standing outside it, hoping at least a few of them had special ops training in some form or another.

CHAPTER 21

STALKING THE CAT

Sherman Oaks, CA

BOBBY SENT MEREDETH a text, then secured his phone and drew his pistol again, keeping his movements small, slow, invisible. He raised his gaze back to the roof of the building across the intersection and raked it from one end of the building to the other. A low-volume whistle came from his left—Cliff, no doubt—but he didn't take his eyes off the roof.

He knew Meredeth would muster an assault team and come running, and he was counting on that. It would surely flush any suspicious character out of hiding—or at least get him moving instead of waiting and watching.

The night was a black one; only a sliver of the moon showed its face, and clouds contributed to the darkness. Bobby continued to stare at the rooftop, but it was like trying to distinguish a black object against a black backdrop.

The low whistle came again, closer this time.

"Don't burn my position," he hissed.

"What is it?"

"Building across Coldwater Canyon," he whispered. "Take cover. Use the Q45." Cliff hustled back across the street and crouched at the front of the vehicle. Nothing on the rooftop moved, but Bobby wasn't entirely sure he'd spot it if something did.

He heard the battle rattle of an oncoming group, and so did the suspect across the street. A dark figure lunged up out of a prone position, turned, and ran north toward the end of the building as far from Coldwater Canyon Avenue as was possible. "Go, go, go!" Bobby called at Cliff, and then he was up and sprinting toward the building, running flat out but weaving from side to side as his training dictated. Some part of his tactical brain heard Cliff's pounding footsteps, but he didn't glance back. He kept his gaze glued to the edge of the building, readying himself to dive for cover should a rifle barrel slide into sight.

The oncoming group of cops led by Meredeth drew nearer, running across the bridge over the L.A. River, and their battle rattle told Bobby they were coming prepared for a fight. It also offered him a little support in terms of noise that would mask his movements. He darted across the traffic lanes without pausing, though at o-dark-thirty in the morning, there weren't all that many cars to begin with.

Bobby cleared the curb and most of the accompanying sidewalk in a single bound, glanced left-right-left, and veered toward the gate securing the exit to the building's underground parking. He found that secured, however, then continued past the "Now Leasing" sign and pounded down a flight of concrete steps after checking the corner with a quick glance. At the bottom of the steps, the walkway paralleled the river, though it led to a high gated barrier lit by an old-fashioned-looking coach light.

There was a door to the left, and given its location, he guessed it led to the parking garage. He tried the handle and found it locked, as well. He turned to the gated barrier, eyeing its height, then grasped the knob on the gate and pulled hard. The gate popped open, almost sending him ass-over-teakettle, and he stumbled through it. "Gate on the south side! Pull *hard*!" he yelled over his shoulder.

"Ten-four!" yelled McCloe.

Behind Bobby, Cliff's footsteps pounding down the concrete steps echoed back and forth across the concrete channel of the L.A. River, followed by a clang— the gate. "Let the others know by radio!"

"On it!" shouted Cliff, and Bobby heard the susurration of his radio message.

Bobby cleared his mind, letting go of the desire to make sure Cliff had gotten the message out, letting go of his worry for Meredeth, and ran flat out down the cement path that edged the south side of the building. Most of the lights set at the level of the second story were out—

smashed or burnt out or simply turned off to save energy. Bobby didn't know which, but he slowed as he approached the corner of the building, which stood illuminated by a single commercial-grade light.

The cone of light bothered him, and he slowed further, regaining his breath and trying to pierce the white glare and see beyond it. If he were the one being pursued, he'd have used that cone (even if he had to shoot out the preceding lights to create it) as an ambush. He proceeded at a speed just above a fast walk but bent at the waist to lower his target profile. He ran closer and closer to the wall until his shoulder brushed the gray-painted stucco. Four yards from the wash of brilliance, he slowed to a stop and squatted on his hunkers, his gaze welded to the darkness on the other side of the sea of white light.

He could sense nothing over there, no movement, no hinky feeling, no nothing. Cliff's pounding footfalls sounded behind him, and he stuck his right arm out, palm down, and waved it up and down. He duckwalked forward, his pistol held at ready, his Glock's muzzle pointed at that cone of light, ready to press the gun out into an Isosceles firing position at a moment's notice. He felt, rather than sensed, McCloe taking a position behind him providing high cover. The two men moved forward at a snail's pace, waiting for the fight to kick off.

The night had turned silent without even the omnipresent sound of crickets and other nocturnal insects. Bobby edged forward and extended his arms to raise the sights into his visual plane. Cliff rested his left hand on Bobby's right shoulder and gave a little squeeze, telling him Cliff was ready to follow in high cover.

Far behind them, the gate clanked and clattered as many booted feet pounded through it. Bobby lunged through the cone of bright light and rounded the corner, Cliff right on his heels. They stopped in a mulched planting bed, discovering the sidewalk slanted toward the narrower end of the building. All the lights from that point to the end of the walk were out. At the far end, Bobby could just make out another concrete stairwell that led upward to a gated barrier and, beyond that, the top of another staircase that followed the east edge of the building.

He hesitated a moment, his gaze tracking his pistol as he examined the planting area that filled the triangle between the building and the far end. There were two areas of concern: an awning-covered entrance to the parking garage and, just past the stairs that led up to the gate, what looked like a door to a maintenance and landscaping equipment room.

He heard the battle clatter of Meredeth and her team slowing down for the light. He turned his head and called, "Clear!" as he rose from his crouch and returned his pistol to high ready.

Meredeth came around the corner cautiously, with six LASD deputies in tow. "What's the story?" she whispered.

"I couldn't get in the parking garage. This seemed like the next best way to the back."

"Okay. What—"

An engine roared to life in the east, sounding close, and Bobby sprinted toward the stairs, pounding up the flight, slammed the gate open, then skipped the downward set of steps and instead jumped the railing. He hit hard, but that was nothing new to him. He sprinted toward the blacktop he could see through the brush, Meredeth and the deputies thundering along the path above and behind him.

Branches and leaves slapped at this face, and he ducked the ones he could but never took his eyes off that sliver of roadway. A dark car streaked down the road, and Bobby pushed his way out of the bushes, set himself in an Isosceles stance, and pushed the gun out, taking up the trigger's slack as he did so. He followed the car with the Glock's snout, but there were residential homes in the backdrop, and without knowing the car's driver was the unsub, he couldn't justify taking the risk. The car screeched through a lefthand turn and was gone.

CHAPTER 22

NARROW ESCAPES

Sherman Oaks, CA

DRUITT SWUNG THE big Cutlass left, his gaze darting back and forth between the rearview mirrors and the image of Connelly's guard dog leveling a pistol at him and the road. The big block engine under the hood howled as he hammered the accelerator down the residential street, but he had no choices left. The pursuit had been too close. If he'd been another few minutes descending the stairs and getting to the car, Van Zandt would have been all over him.

He shook his head and flicked on his police scanner, listening for the inevitable BOLO call and the LASD's tactics for containing him, for boxing him in until an air unit could get eyes on him. He turned up the volume without looking, one hand at twelve o'clock on the steering wheel. He reached the intersection of Goodland and Woodbridge and thundered through it without so much as twitching his foot away from the floor. When

Goodland Avenue dead-ended into Bloomfield Street, he flipped the Oldsmobile sedan to the right and roared toward Belaire Avenue, putting distance and a residential neighborhood between himself and any jackleg pursuers from Dark Annie's resting spot.

Better be smart, bucko, he thought in a mental voice that hissed like sandpaper on rusty steel. *You may know these streets like the back of your hand, but the cops have radios, and radio waves are faster than any car.*

He brushed the thought aside, wrenching the four-door to the left, grimacing as the Cutlass's rear end hopped and shivered. He fed the car more gas, and the rear end straightened out. He raced north to Moorpark Street, then headed east again. He figured if he could get to Whitsett Avenue before the first radio call, his success was virtually guaranteed.

Just as he was slowing for the right-hander onto Whitsett, the call went out: "*Attention, all cars! Attention, all cars! Be on the lookout for a mid-Eighties Oldsmobile Cutlass, dark colored, four-door, license plate unknown. Last seen in the vicinity of Goodland Avenue and Valleyheart Drive east of Coldwater Canyon Avenue. Suspect is believed armed and extremely dangerous. Do not initiate contact without backup. Notify dispatch immediately.*"

"Too late," he said with a grin. He turned left on Whitsett and drove south at a stately pace, his lights on, obeying every traffic rule. He had only six or seven blocks to go. His grin widened as he imagined Connelly's face when she got the news he'd escaped. It wasn't as fun as imagining how he would take her life, but it was good, nonetheless.

He cruised down Whittset and passed over the L.A. River, then turned left on Ventura, then left again on Granville. He idled down the partial block to Ventura Court and turned right—toward the automobile entrance of the storage place where he kept his "work" cars. He had six, so the BOLO status of the Cutlass wouldn't slow him down.

Not at all.

CHAPTER 23

JACK AND KILL

David Branch's Farm, NY

CARL LEANED BACK, clicking the recliner into a more relaxed position as Michelina walked toward him. He patted his thigh and smiled up at her, and she grinned back as she slid into his lap. She kissed him on the lips— nothing sexy, just a quick hello peck, and he slid his arm around her waist.

"Did you hear Jack at dinner?" she asked.

"Yeah."

"What do you think?"

"He's a liar. A poser. Father or Alex will sort him out."

"Do you think so? They aren't omniscient, after all."

"You could have fooled me," he said with a slight smile. "Anyway, slapping Jack back into his proper place isn't my job."

"Father didn't punish you for Jonathon, did he?"

"No."

"And Alex?"

"She was there. She told me to do it."

"And that doesn't tell you how much respect you've earned from both of them?"

"Well..."

"Well, nothing, Carl. It used to be that Alex was Father's enforcer, but as you guys got bigger and bigger and bigger—"

"Wait, are we still talking about Jack?" He grinned.

"We'll have *that* discussion later when we have more privacy."

"I'm going to hold you to it." He waggled his eyebrows.

"No, you better hold it to me." She laughed deep in her throat, and Carl's temperature seemed to spike upward. "But I mean in physical size and strength—it was clear to everyone that if you or Mack decided to fight Alex, it would go badly. Haven't you noticed he's far less physical than he once was? At least toward you giants?"

"No," he said, "I hadn't. Alex was the one who beat Lucy up. He told me Lucy probably instigated him for that very purpose. She wanted a beating that would leave marks, wanted something that would enrage me."

"I'm sure Jonathon would agree that she accomplished what the manipulative little bitch set out to do," said Michelina in a cold, cold voice. "And now she's got her hooks in Jack."

"Yeah," said Carl. "But what can I do about it?"

"You can tell him what she's up to."

"He won't believe me. She'll be whispering in his ear the whole time. She's probably already inoculated him from my influence." He rolled his gaze up to the ceiling and rested his head on the back of the chair.

"Start out by calling him on his B.S. Let him know that liars are treated poorly around here. And if Lucy happens to hear that message, even better."

"What, just walk up to him and say, 'you've never killed anyone, sport. Stop lying about it?'"

"Why not?"

"Because Jack's a guy. He'll take that as a challenge, and I'll end up having to pound him. Everyone will think it's because of Lucy."

"Who cares what the others think?"

Carl shrugged his shoulders. "I just don't think it's a good idea."

"Okay," Michelina said with a shrug.

"What? That's it? You're not going to try to argue? You're not going to bully me?"

"Oh, Carl. You wasted too much time with that little shrew."

"I guess I did," he said.

"If you have my back, I'm not afraid to call him out. And I'm a girl, so he won't get his macho bent out of shape."

"Maybe," said Carl. "I've got your back, Michelina, you don't have to worry about that."

"I know, but I wanted your tacit approval. I didn't want you to think I manipulated you."

"Believe me, I'm a pro at spotting manipulation now. When do you want to do this?"

"The sooner the better." She squealed as Carl stood up, lifting her from his lap and curling her into his arms as he did so. "Wow," she said a little breathlessly.

He grinned at her and set her on her feet. "Where is he?" he asked.

"Up in the machine shed, last I saw him."

"Come on, then." He held out his hand, and Michelina dropped hers into his. They walked up the hill hand in hand, and when they reached the crown, they found Lucy staring at them through narrowed eyelids from where she leaned against the corner of the building.

"Hi, Lucy," said Michelina brightly. "Is Jack still inside?"

With a typical teenage girl's eye roll, she waved her hand toward the building's roll-up doors. "See for yourself. I'm not his keeper."

"No?" asked Carl without looking at her. "Do you think he'd say the same?"

With a huff and a curled lip, Lucy pushed away from the building and rounded the corner. Michelina and Carl followed her, and Carl couldn't keep the small curl of a smile off his lips.

Only one of the big roll-up doors stood open. The one where Mack's truck had been parked was closed. "Think he'll be back?" Carl asked softly.

"No," said Michelina. "One way or another, he's gone for good. He told me as much."

"Ah," said Carl.

"Jack! The grown-ups are here!" called Lucy as she crossed the threshold into the machine shed.

Carl's lips twisted, but Michelina only smiled with one side of her mouth. "Ah, jealousy," she said with a laugh as they walked into the building. "Will you turn green, too, Lucy?"

"What?" asked Lucy, brows drawn down, her flinty gaze flickering between Carl and Michelina.

Michelina laughed and shook her head. She turned to Jack, the beanpole of a kid who'd come out of his box only a few weeks earlier. "What's this I hear about your first kill, Jack?"

He puffed out his non-existent chest and nodded. "That's right. Father took me into town for my test before him and Mack—"

"I don't think so," said Michelina. "You don't have to lie to us, Jack. In fact, you probably don't want to let any untrue word dribble from your mouth. Father expects us to be honest with one another."

As she'd spoken, Jack's face had suffused with blood, and his eyes flicked back and forth between her and Carl. "I'm not lying!"

Carl couldn't resist a knowing chuckle, but Michelina only sighed. "It seems like you came out of the box too early. Maybe I'll speak to Alex."

"You won't say a word if you don't want to get hurt."

Carl stepped around Michelina and walked up to Jack, towering over him. "Why? Who's going to hurt her?" He bent down to put his nose within an inch of Jack's. "You, twerp?"

"She doesn't scare me, and neither do you." Even so, Jack's gaze darted toward Lucy.

"Bull," said Carl. "Everyone and everything on this farm scares you."

"That's not true."

"Yes, it is." Carl straightened and stepped back to Michelina's side. "And you should know, I've got Michelina's back. She's my friend, and I don't let anyone cause trouble for my friends." As he spoke the last sentence, his gaze slid to meet Lucy's blazing glare. "*Anyone.*"

"Jack," said Michelina, "Father didn't take you into town. You're not ready for town, and everyone who's taken one of Father's trips knows that just by looking at you."

"Shut up!" he all but squealed.

"Leave him alone!" snapped Lucy.

Michelina turned to the small girl, and her expression darkened. "You've done Jack a disservice with your manipulative crap, Lucy. Do you want him to get killed, too?"

Lucy dropped her gaze to the gravel floor of the shed. "Shut up," she muttered.

"See, Jack? You should know who your girlfriend really is, and what she really wants from you. It might be she wants to trick you into killing someone for her." Michelina rested her hand on Carl's shoulder, even though she had to reach up to do it. Jack's gaze darted toward Lucy, and

Michelina sighed. "You see? Carl would *destroy* you, kid. Can't you see he's bigger, stronger, faster, better trained, older, and *actually experienced* in taking lives? You'd get slaughtered. What's more, Lucy knows it. She doesn't care about you, not in the least."

"Yes, she does! She told me she loves me!"

"Jesus, kid, did you just fall off the turnip truck?"

"You shut up!" He took a threatening step forward.

Carl stepped up to meet his advance. "*She's using you, Jack!* Take it from someone who knows how manipulative she is."

"No." The boy shook his head.

"Did she tell you about us?" Carl asked in a low voice. "Did she tell you how she had sex with me, how she dressed as slutty as Father would allow until I noticed her? Did she tell you that she told me she loved me *every* day? Multiple times per day? Did she tell you *why* she did all that? Did she tell you—"

"*Shut up!*" snapped Lucy from behind him.

"—how she got Alex mad so that he'd beat her, then came running to me and claimed Jonathon had raped her? That *he'd* been the one to beat her up? How she egged me on, stoked the fire of my rage until I was ready to snap? Did she tell you any of that?"

Jack's brows bunched, and he turned his gaze on Lucy. "Luce? Who's Jonathon? Is he away with Father, too?"

"He *did* rape me!" Lucy cried.

"No, he didn't," said Carl. "Jack, listen to me. Jonathon's not around anymore. She wound and wound and wound me up until I couldn't see straight for all the rage. She tricked me into cutting Jonathon's heart out. That's why you don't know him. He's dead and buried." He flung his hand toward the fallow field between the house and the machine shed. "He's out there, buried in an unmarked grave. No casket, no clothes. *Worm food.* And I'll tell you something else: Lucy'll get you killed. She's already put you on the path to the gallows—except Father never kills anyone in such a mundane way." He shook his head. "He may have Alex do it, or maybe me, instead, but however he decides to do it, it will be bloody, and it will *hurt.* Get me?"

Jack's frown intensified, and his gaze darted from Carl to Michelina to Lucy and then started around the circle again.

"Jack, don't listen to these lies," said Lucy. She stepped to his side and laced her fingers between his. "Can't you see how jealous Carl is? I *dumped* him when I realized how wrapped around Michelina's finger he was. How he hung on Father's every word, every gesture, hoping he'd find some hint of praise in it. It's sad, but Carl's just broken. I want to be with a *real* man."

Michelina laughed and shook her head. "Come on, Jack, you've got to see that for what it is."

He narrowed his eyes at her. "Leave me alone. You're not my mother! You're not my sister!"

"Tell them, baby," said Lucy with a victorious smile bending her lips.

"And *you*, too," he snapped, jerking his hand from hers and stomping out of the machine shed.

"You bastard!" Lucy hissed at Carl. "Can't you leave me alone?"

"You first. Stop trying to recruit new kids to kill me."

She scoffed, then spat on the ground. "As if!"

CHAPTER 24

TAKING A STAB AT A PROFILE

Sherman Oaks, CA

THEY STUCK AROUND the crime scene until the ME's crime scene investigators packed the decedent into a black body bag and loaded it into their vehicle for transfer back to the morgue. With each passing moment, Meredeth's hopes for an easy capture of the unsub died a little more until there was no hope left. There had been no sightings of any older model Oldsmobile Cutlasses by anyone, law enforcement or civilian.

"We had a rolling perimeter up in ten minutes," said Cliff McCloe, shaking his head. "How did he evade us?"

"Simple," said Bobby. "His base is within ten minutes of here."

"That or he drove fast enough to get out of the area," said Meredeth.

Still shaking his head, Cliff said, "Who is this guy? We were *right here*, and he risked *everything* to watch us at the scene. I mean, that's...that's..." He shook his head harder.

"It's unusual, to say the least," said Meredeth. "As to who this guy is, I might have my first take on that."

"A profile?" asked Cliff.

"Yes, but for now, I don't want it shared with anyone who's not sitting in the car with us."

"But Roger—"

"*Anyone*, she said." Bobby turned around in the seat and faced her. "I'm assuming this is a provisional profile?"

"It is," she said, "and it might be inaccurate, Cliff, but that's not why I want to exclude Roger. As of right now, he's a suspect."

"What? No way! Roger's—"

"He's a suspect in that we have to exclude him after this morning's A.W.O.L."

"But he's just... He has trouble sleeping. Sometimes he's up for so long he can't wake up."

"Even so, nothing I say here goes to Roger. Clear?"

Cliff shook his head but said, "Crystal clear, but I have to register my objections and say that I think you're way off base. Roger's a cop!"

"He is, but that doesn't mean he's above suspicion," said Bobby.

"I've known him for—"

"Cliff, did you follow the Ankou case? The .40 Caliber Killer?" asked Meredeth.

McCloe nodded. "What was in the paper, anyway."

"Then you know we have no idea who Ankou really is. He has no DNA or fingerprint records, and so far, no one's called the tip line with a hint at his true identity."

"I don't see—"

Meredeth held up her hand like a traffic cop telling McCloe to stop. "Listen to me, Cliff, and don't interrupt. Ankou was far more active than the media—or the FBI for that matter—knew. Oh, not the recent murders—we got him for those."

"That's right," said Bobby. "But he's also the most likely candidate for a string of murder-kidnappings that occurred twenty years ago."

"He killed everyone in the house except for the teenagers or preteens he kidnapped, one to a house. But he didn't kill those children. In essence, he adopted them, but in his world, there's nothing wrong with inflicting psychological and physical torture. He used a process called 'psychic driving' to reshape those children into his own image."

"That sounds crazy."

Meredeth nodded. "It does at that. And at first, we didn't believe his claims." She rubbed the part of her belly that still felt tight, the internal and external scar tissue from her emergency surgery and subsequent temporary ileostomy. "Then we met one of those kids. His first-born son, he said, though the unsub was biologically female."

"He rewrote her personality," said Bobby. "Convinced her that to be female was to be unreliable, overly emotional, and illogical."

"So that poor girl convinced herself she was male despite the physical evidence. A created transgender."

Bobby grinned, but it wasn't a pleasant sight to behold. "And that's not all. He made her into a brutal serial killer. He started her off on her murder spree when she was young—fourteen or so, we think. And he had other children there as well."

"But...*why*?" asked Cliff, his face drawn into a moue of disgust and bewilderment.

"He had a long-term goal," said Meredeth.

"Yeah?"

Meredeth nodded. "And one that was influenced by my brother, whom I didn't remember until on the Ankou case."

"Whoa," murmured Cliff. "And what is this plan?"

"To teach me a lesson," she said with a shrug. "If he has his way, it will most likely be the last lesson I ever learn."

"But..." Cliff looked out the windshield and shook his head. "What does all this have to do with the unsub in this case?"

"Cliff, Ankou had over twenty years in which to kidnap children and perfect his methods. He wasn't even on anyone's radar. Imagine how many kids we could be talking about."

"A thousand. More."

"That's right," said Bobby. "But what Meredeth hasn't told you is that his plan to teach her a lesson includes sending his 'children' out into the world to perfect their techniques, then to carry out his instructions once the time is right."

"And the signal that the time was right was his capture and conviction," said Meredeth. "That's why we didn't meet Alex—his first-born—until after he was imprisoned. Alex's cover was as a female ADA in Pinellas County. In her guise, Alex requested Bobby and my help on a case."

"A series of kidnap-murders that Alex committed," said Bobby.

"That's right. The request for our assistance was a ploy to get me to St. Petersburg, Florida. Alex wanted a direct competition—him against us." Meredeth shook her head.

"And we were hard on his trail, but that's what almost killed Meredeth."

Cliff turned to gaze at her, his eyebrows arched.

"Stabbed me right in the guts," she said in a voice so low it was almost a whisper, and her hand crept back to her scar. "He'd been with us all day, in his female persona. We found one of his safe houses, and in the garage, we found an expensive Porsche 911." She shrugged. "I smashed the window with a hammer, and that set him off. He attacked from behind; he directed my attention to the neighborhood, then pulled a knife and jammed it into my guts." She closed her eyes and fell silent.

"But I heard the commotion," said Bobby. "I hit Alex hard enough to send him sprawling on the driveway and we got Meredeth to the hospital."

"But that's not the point," said Meredeth. "Yes, we caught Alex, but his part in the plan had been to go first, to start dropping bodies with Ankou's signature carved into their dead flesh."

"A Trinity Celtic Knot," added Bobby.

"Yes. Then we faced a vigilante in the form of a truck driver—and he got away."

"Right, he's in hiding as far as we can tell."

"But during the course of that case, we were contacted by another of Ankou's children—a woman who had fooled Ankou and Alex into believing she was as mentally changed as Alex but who had broken from the fold instead. She'd gone underground and, as far as we know, none of the Ankou kids could find her. Her name is Michelina, and she's the source of a lot of our knowledge."

"Okay," said Cliff.

"She told us that one of Ankou's tribe was in law enforcement," said Bobby.

"At least one, she said."

Cliff gave a low whistle. "Okay, I get why that could make you suspicious. But why do you think this case has anything to do with Ankou?"

"Let me tell you about our last case," said Bobby. "It was also in California but up north. Ukiah. We thought we were doing our boss a favor. That we were looking into the disappearance of his nephew."

"I wish that's all it was," said Meredeth.

"Instead, we found a serial killer who'd been running under the radar for two decades. We're not sure how long he was active."

"And he was one of these children?"

"No, he was just a poor guy with mental health issues. He was manipulated by one of Ankou's children, though. A woman named Lucy. She drove the poor guy even farther away from reality."

"Convinced him to stop taking his meds."

"Convinced him he was a priest of Satan."

"Um, okay."

"The point is, she was part of the plan, too, and our boss's nephew was likely the reason she was in Ukiah to begin with. She probably whispered poison into Kahin's ear and fed his rage until he killed the poor kid."

"How..."

"How did we know? We didn't until it came time to raid the house. In the basement, we found the Trinity Knot. At first, we thought this Kahin character was one of the kids, but it wasn't him. It was Lucy."

"Then all three..."

"Now you're catching on," said Bobby. "All of Meredeth's cases since we locked him up have led back to Ankou."

"And Michelina said the plan is a long one. Ankou plans to lead me around by the nose, from one of his brainwashed killers to the next until one of them wins the competition."

"And kills you?" asked Cliff.

"I don't think so," said Meredeth.

"It could be Meredeth is right, but remember she spoke of her estranged brother? Michelina told us he served as an 'uncle' figure to the kids at Ankou's farm, that his rage for Meredeth has been stoked by Ankou."

"And Ankou wants you dead? He wants his kids to kill you for your brother?"

"We're not sure about that," said Meredeth. "But I imagine my brother will be involved in whatever happens next."

Cliff let loose with another low whistle. "This Michelina woman said at least one of the other kids is now in law enforcement. I get that, but why Roger?"

Bobby nodded. "Because he wasn't here last night. He's not here *now*."

"And—"

"But I told you he doesn't sleep well."

"*And*," repeated Meredeth, "he trips some of my internal alarms. And he fits this initial profile, at least in part."

"Then let's hear it," said Cliff. "I'm sure I'll be able to explain the things that concern you."

"Fine. Our unsub is likely middle-aged, perhaps thirty to fifty. He's got a job but one with flexible hours. He's strong, probably big, rugged. He dresses well, nothing wild that would stand out, nothing offensive. He's a loner through and through and prefers to be alone rather than be in the company of *anyone* else, male or female. He's single as a result. He's eccentric. Most people would describe him as a little odd, a little stand-offish. He's irritable in the company of others. He lives in or around Sherman Oaks but has at least a storage unit large enough to hide the car. He knows the area very well. He drives a dark-colored personal car but, again, nothing flashy. Utilitarian, yes, but nothing bling or souped up."

Cliff grimaced and opened his mouth, but then he closed it without saying a word. He turned back to the front and sat, shoulder's slumped, looking straight ahead. Neither Bobby nor Meredeth spoke, leaving the detective to his thoughts, but they both knew the profile described Roger Shelton to a tee. After a few minutes of silence, Cliff started the engine. "Let's get back to the station."

"Better idea," said Meredeth. "Let's go to Roger's house. After that, the ME's office."

"Right," said Cliff.

CHAPTER 25

UNDER THE RADAR

Sherman Oaks, CA

DRUITT MANEUVERED THE Cutlass to the back of the extra-large storage unit, putting his five other "work" cars between the Cutlass and any curious employee of the storage place or any citizen who happened to be walking by as he entered or exited the unit. Then he threw an old tarp over the car for further camouflage.

He took off his black shirt, jacket, and gloves but left on the black canvas pants. No one would think anything about a guy wearing black work pants. He slipped into a T-shirt, then slid his arms through the sleeves of an old button-up he kept there for just such an occasion. He entered the closet-sized bathroom and stared at himself in the mirror, checking that he hadn't missed any telltale splotches of Dark Annie's blood or tissue.

He returned to the large main room, flipped open the case his Liston knives lived in, then set about cleaning all three of them with methodical concentration. He first washed them, then treated them with Tergazyme powder and water—a chemical cleaner designed to remove protein, body fluids, and tissue from metals. Then he mixed a small portion of Alconox and bleach to break up any RNA that had wormed its way into the fixtures and preheated it in the microwave and set the knives into a metal pan to soak in the solution, then moved the pan into the toaster oven he'd purchased for the purpose. He'd have to come back in a few hours and clean the knives with Citranox to kill any stray DNA.

He didn't like being without the Liston knives, but it wasn't as if he could interrupt his day to go murder a slut. And the knives would be pretty useless against Connelly and her pit bull. The news articles out of St. Petersburg had proven that beyond the shadow of a doubt.

He flicked on the internal light of the little toaster oven and looked in at his Liston set with a slight smile on his face. He had so many fond memories. After all, Mary Ann Blocker hadn't been his first, and Dark Annie wouldn't be his last.

He exited the storage unit and walked down to the parking lot where he'd parked his daily driver, then headed west on Ventura Boulevard.

CHAPTER 26
A.W.O.L.
Los Angeles, CA

CLIFF'S MOBILE PHONE rang as he turned west on Ventura. He glanced at the caller ID and grunted, "Shelton." He accepted the call and put it on speaker. "Where have you been?"

"I had a bad night. I got up late, but I've eaten and am ready to go to work."

"Roger..."

"What? And why am I on speaker? You know I hate that."

"I'm driving. You'll just have to deal with it. Where are you now?"

"I thought of something to check, so I went down to Kindred Haven and had a look."

"Yeah?" asked Bobby. "What?"

"It turned out to be nothing. A waste of time. I'm at the courthouse, Cliff. Come get me."

"We need to talk, Rog. This disappearing act of yours has gotten old. I'm tired of covering for you all the time."

The line hissed a moment, then Shelton said, "Come get me," and hung up.

"He's pleasant," said Meredeth.

"Yeah," said Cliff with a grimace. "He hates to be called out on anything, so he's going to be even weirder today than he was yesterday."

"I'm not sure that's possible," said Bobby.

"Just wait... Yesterday was a good day for Shelton," said Cliff. He turned north on Van Nuys Boulevard and shook his head at the traffic. "Don't tell anyone," he said as he flicked on the Impala's blue lights and blipped his siren to get the first row of cars out of his way. They drove in silence, each lost in whatever thoughts they could muster after a short sleep and an action-filled early morning.

Meredeth pinched the bridge of her nose, but more out of habit than in an effort to alleviate a headache. She didn't like not knowing if they had another wolf in sheep's clothing in their midst. Her guts seemed to pulse with fear, and phantom pain ripped across her midsection. Bobby sat in front of her, his gaze on the traffic ahead of them. He'd gotten pretty close to the unsub—he would have had him if not for the houses down range. She knew it irked him, being stymied like that, but no one else would ever read his annoyance through that stone-like face he'd developed.

McCloe turned right on Delano, then pulled into the gated lot for the building the Sheriff's Department shared with Los Angeles Superior Court. Roger paced back and forth in front of the doorway to the building, his face pulled down into a moue. He had his hands behind his back, and his posture was slightly hunched as if he expected someone to sneak up on him and box his ears.

Cliff swung the Impala into one of the spots reserved for the disabled and blipped the horn. Roger started, then jogged over while Bobby got out and slid into the back seat with Meredeth. Shelton sat down and pulled his long legs into the car, then slammed the door. He glanced at Cliff and rolled his fingers in the canonical "let's get going" gesture.

Shaking his head, McCloe backed out of the parking spot and headed back toward the street. "I could do with breakfast. Anyone else?"

"I could eat," said Bobby.

"Of course you can," said Meredeth. "You're awake."

"Har-har."

"I've already eaten," said Roger, and the atmosphere turned chilly. "Tell me about this latest crime. Did you get a look at the suspect?" he asked, then turned to Bobby and arched an eyebrow.

"I did," Bobby said.

"Oh? And can you describe him?"

"Can you?"

Roger knotted his brows and frowned. "How could I? I missed all the fun this morning. Have you forgotten?"

"No, I haven't. Why break the schedule? Why pick up a woman at random?"

Shelton looked at him for another few silent seconds, then glanced at Meredeth before turning his attention to McCloe. "I feel like I've missed something."

"You definitely have," said Cliff, and his tone wasn't much warmer than Bobby's.

Roger gave him a bewildered stare for a few moments, then turned and speared Meredeth with an intense gaze. "Agent Connelly, will you tell me what's going on?"

"It's simple, Roger. Last night you...*your* unsub took another life. Cliff was unable to wake you, so you weren't there when I examined the body in situ."

"And you weren't there when Van Zandt and I spotted the unsub watching us from a nearby rooftop."

"You did?"

"Yes, we did, Roger," said Cliff in the same cold tone. "We gave chase, as well. We almost caught him, but he was a handful of seconds faster than us, and he made his escape. If you'd been listening to the radio, you'd know there's a BOLO out on him and the dark-colored Cutlass he was driving."

"Good. Then we'll have him in custody by—"

"Nah, nah. He got away clean. No sightings by civilians or cops."

"Oh," said Roger.

"What kind of car do you drive, Shelton?" asked Bobby. His tone gave the seemingly informal question a great deal of gravitas.

"A Mazda CX9. Why?"

"What color?"

"Dark blue. Why are you asking me about my car?"

"Oh, no reason," said Bobby. "All this talk of cars just got me wondering."

"Uh-huh," murmured Roger. "Look, all of you. I'm sorry my sleep issues put a burr under your blankets, but things happen. Can't we just let it go?"

"Beyond the wasted time explaining the scene and the events to you in detail, I really don't care," said Meredeth. "*If*, that is, you were really asleep."

"I said as much, didn't I?" he asked, but his tone held no pique, no annoyance, just confusion.

"Yeah, you did," said Cliff. "There's still some question about veracity, though."

"Cliff, you and I..." Roger shook his head. "I don't understand. Why would you doubt me?"

Cliff nodded once, then recited Meredeth's profile nearly word for word. When he was finished, he gave Roger a pointed look. "Sound familiar to you?"

Roger looked at each of them in turn, his face set in stone. Finally, he turned his gaze back to Cliff, and a large smile spread across his face. "It sounds a lot like me." He laughed aloud. "Am I a *suspect*?" His eyes danced a little as he asked the question.

"Look, Roger—"

"Roger," said Meredeth in a soft voice that made each man strain to hear her. "Look at me, please."

Roger swiveled in his seat and met her gaze head-on. "Yes?"

"It's not unusual for a cop involved in the investigation to fit an initial profile. In fact, on one of our cases, Bobby suspected the chief of police—who was entirely innocent. So let's say you're not a suspect yet, but you *are* someone we have to exclude from the investigation. I don't suppose you have an alibi for last night? A girlfriend, maybe?"

Shelton grinned at her, but it was without humor. "Like your profile says, I'm a loner and prefer to keep myself to myself. No alibi."

"How about this morning? Can anyone at the hospital confirm when you arrived and when you left?"

"I imagine the security cameras can." His voice was flat, emotionless, but his right eyelid twitched. "I can't believe you didn't stand up for me, McCloe," he said, turning back to his partner.

"He did," said Bobby, "but even he's confused as to how you could fit the profile so exactly."

"You described every person in my group," said Roger. "*Exactly.* Your profile may seem to point only at me, but to my mind, it's generalized to the point of uselessness." He cocked his head to the side as if thinking. "Except for the car and color. Why dark color?"

Meredeth pumped one shoulder up and down. "The unsub seems to enjoy ambush and stealth. Plus, a dark car without its lights on is nearly invisible at night. It makes the car harder to spot, both while driving and when parked.

"Yes, I see. But why is my *personal* car so important."

"Serial killers often use their personal cars when stalking their victims. They don't use the car they will use at the time of the abduction because they don't want the victim spotting the car during the stalk and again right before the abduction or murder. Alarmed victims are unpredictable. It's the same for the flash factor and exhaust note. Serial killers prefer not being noticed."

"Ah, I see. And why else might someone buy a dark-colored car?"

"They like the color, or maybe it was the only car available with the features they wanted."

"Yes. Yes, *exactly,*" said Roger. "Would you honestly say my job has flexible hours?"

"Not so much," said Bobby. "But the fact of the matter is, you don't seem much bothered by the fact that you slept through the investigation and action this morning."

Roger wagged his head from side to side. "There's nothing anyone can do about the past. It's dead and gone, so there's no reason to be upset by it."

Cliff scoffed and swung the Impala into the parking lot of The Carb Café, pulled into a spot close to the door, and killed the engine. "Yeah? Is that how it is, Roger?" he asked in a voice that shook.

"Yes, it is. I can't go back and make sure I wake up for your call. I can't—"

"You're forgetting one thing, Shelton," said Cliff.

"Oh? What's that?"

"I left you *multiple* messages. If you'd listened to them at all, you'd have come to the crime scene instead of messing around at Kindred Haven—*if* that's what you really did." He opened his door and climbed out of the car, but then he bent and stuck his head inside. "Now, I'm hungry. I'm going inside to order breakfast, and all of you are invited, but if my company is too much for you, you can sit out here in the car." He straightened and closed the door—not quite slamming it, but it was a football field away from gently.

"I could eat," said Bobby as he opened his own door and got out.

"Coming, Roger?" Meredeth asked.

"No. Not hungry, and this place sucks."

Meredeth shrugged, got out, and followed McCloe and Van Zandt inside.

CHAPTER 27

I HATE LUCY

David Branch's Farm, NY

CARL YAWNED, STRETCHED, and scratched himself, then headed for one of the three upstairs bathrooms, hoping he could get in, perform his ablutions, and get out before the gaggle of new kids got up and started their daily program of screaming and laughing. He was a little sore from what happened after the confrontation in the machine shed. Michelina had made good on her promise. A little grin surfaced on his lips as he thought of the celebration out in the trees.

Father was due back soon, and Carl needed a good scrubbing, a shave, and maybe a trim of his dark locks. He hoped Michelina could help him with his hair, and he hoped getting up early had granted him exclusive access to one of the bathrooms. He walked toward the closest one, but the door was closed, and a sliver of light stabbed at the relative darkness in the hall. He approached the door and knocked on it softly. "Done soon?" he asked through the door. The occupant didn't speak, but he heard the water in the sink, the soap dispenser, and then the water stopped. The door rattled—the lock's release—and swung open.

Lucy stood inside the bathroom, but she didn't look up to meet his gaze. "I was going to take a shower. You're welcome to join me."

"I don't think that's a good idea," he said, keeping his voice low, calm.

She nodded her head once—a gesture he knew all too well—then glared up at him. "You know what *I* don't think is a good idea?"

Shaking his head, Carl turned to go check the other bathrooms, but Lucy's iron grip snapped over his wrist, and she pulled him around to face her. She pulled him *hard*. "I'll tell you! I don't think it's a good idea for you to cross me like you did yesterday. Out in the machine shed? You remember, don't you?"

Carl sighed and shook his wrist to dislodge her grip, but she hung on tight. "Let go, Lucy," he said in an enervated voice. "Let's just agree to live and let live. Sound good?"

"Too late. It's *too late*, Carl. You drove Jack away. He won't have anything to do with me! I went to his room last night wearing only my robe, and do you know what happened?"

"Lucy—"

"He called me a *slut* and *pushed me away*, Carl. And that's your fault."

"Oh, it's my fault? I was the one who tried to manipulate Jack? I'm the one who made up a story about myself, something to get him wound up? That's a load of bull excrement, Luce, and you know it." Using his other hand, he peeled her grip off his wrist. He could have done it regardless of her response, but she allowed him to do it, hanging her head. "All I did was tell the kid the truth. If that drives people away from you, Luce, you should consider a change in ways."

"Sure. Easy. Easy, right?" she said listlessly. "Like I said, it's too late, Carl. Jack told *everyone*. There's no one left for me." She lifted her head and met his gaze. "No one but you. We were meant for each other, Carl. I've been thinking about life after graduation. We could start a cult—use your knowledge of religion to craft a belief system that will attract society's cast-offs. We could set up a place, a compound maybe, and in it, *we* could set the rules. We could do sacrifices—"

"No, Lucy," said Carl. Tears welled in Lucy's eyes, but he didn't know how to determine if she was genuinely crying or if the waterworks were just another tool in Lucy's manipulation arsenal.

She dropped her gaze after a moment's search of his face. "I made a mistake, Carl," she said in a voice full of grief. "I shouldn't have lied to you. Should've just told you the truth, and we could have dealt with Jonathon as a team. It was the only time. I admit I did it. I take responsibility for doing it. I'm just asking you to forgive me. It could be like it was before between us. Better! I'll do anything you ask me to, Carl. *Anything.*"

"Lucy..." Carl sighed and shook his head. "I forgive you, okay? I wish you hadn't done it, and I believe you are truly remorseful. At least as much as any of us can be." She raised her gaze to meet his, and the hope in her eyes made him feel awful. "But as for the rest... It wouldn't work, Lucy. I'd always have this memory in my head, and I'd always question everything you said or did. I'll always be *guarded* around you, Luce. What you did...it cut me to the quick. Do you know that? Have you thought about how I must've felt when I cut out Jonathon's heart for you and then discovered you'd set me up?" He shook his head a second time. "No, things can't go back to the way things were. I'm sorry."

She stood before him, trembling, and finally cut her gaze away from his. "No, I suppose not," she said in that pitiful, wavering voice. "I..." Emotion cut off her voice, and she closed her eyes, tears rushing down her cheeks and diving toward the old wooden floors. She drew a deep breath, pulled her shoulders back, and raised her head. "I won't do anything like Jack again, Carl. I promise. Maybe... Maybe over time you can forget my mistake."

"Maybe," he said aloud. *Never*, he said in his mind.

"Can you do me a favor, though? Please?"

Carl shrugged.

"Could you not rub my face in your relationship with Michelina? Could you take pity on me and give me that one last thing?"

"Lucy, I never intended to rub your face in it. But, I'm not going to sneak around."

"That's more than I deserve," she said mournfully. "Thank you, Carl." She stepped into the hall, and Carl backed up a step.

"No, Luce. I'll use one of the other bathrooms. You don't have to give up your shower."

She turned toward her bedroom but didn't start walking. Her shoulders slumped, and her head fell forward once more. "That's okay. I..." She shook her head. "I don't care about that anymore." She trudged toward her room without looking back.

Carl watched her for a moment, his heart aching, but then he caught himself and purposefully dredged up the memories of how he felt when he discovered her betrayal. Keeping those memories firmly in mind, he turned and entered the bathroom, locking the door behind him.

CHAPTER 28
ENGLISH MUFFINS
Sherman Oaks, CA

BOBBY MADE ELABORATE gestures with his egg-laden fork as he told a story Meredeth had heard at least seventy thousand times. McCloe laughed in all the right places, but she thought his heart wasn't really in it. She dropped her gaze to her own scrambled eggs and three pieces of buttered rye, then opted for her coffee cup instead of adding more to the concrete weight in her stomach. Her head had started to *thud* on the drive over, and she'd hoped the food would help, but even looking at the eggs made her stomach churn. She thought she might be able to stomach the toast despite the butter, but she needed a little time.

"And then Meredeth, as cool as a cucumber, said, 'You're right, of course' in a voice so cold it would have made outer space seem tropical. Then she shut up, her hand on his file, and I thought the guy was about to have a stroke. He *wanted* to look. No, he wanted to grab that file away from her and consume it the way a starving man eats his first meal out of the desert."

"I bet!" said Cliff. He glanced at Meredeth, then cut his gaze back to Van Zandt.

"She went on like that, salting her words with disbelief, playing the hard ass, then dropped it all in a heartbeat and went full-on good cop. I've never seen anyone else pull off *both* roles of good cop bad cop."

"That's something I would pay to see."

"Volusia County Sheriff's Department has it on video. They might share it with you if you asked nicely."

McCloe glanced at Meredeth and smiled, then his gaze darted down to her plate. "Something wrong with your breakfast, Meredeth?"

She showed him a weak smile. "Something wrong with my stomach." She tapped her temple.

"Your head, you mean," said Bobby without lifting his gaze from his plate.

Meredeth hitched both shoulders. "It started on the way over."

"Do you want some Tylenol? I always carry some."

"Thank you but no. I'll take an Excedrin and that'll do the trick." She put a bit of steel into her voice, hoping to stem off any further discussion of her headaches.

"You sure? I can run right out to—"

"I'm sure," she said in a firm voice. She grabbed her bag from the empty chair next to her and started fishing inside for her bottle of caffeine and aspirin.

"Company," Bobby whispered.

Meredeth raised her eyes and looked toward the door. Roger stood just inside and to the right of the glass door. He peered around the place, trying to defeat his daylight-adapted eyes and find them in the dark interior of the café. She raised her arm and waved at him, and his gaze snapped toward the movement. She picked up her bag and put it in her purse so the man would have a place to sit.

As he approached, he nodded at her, a somber expression dominating his face. He pulled out the last free chair and sank into it, his gaze on the table. "Hello."

"Hey, Rog," said McCloe in a voice less hostile than it had been in the car.

"Decide on a bite after all?" asked Bobby.

"Toast, maybe."

Meredeth slid her plate toward him. "You can have mine if you like rye. Or the eggs."

"You're not going to eat them?" Roger asked.

"No, I'll order something else. The idea of the eggs was more appetizing than the plate full of them. Go ahead."

Roger nodded and reached for a triangular wedge of toasted rye. It was already buttered, so he added concord grape jelly and took a bite. "Thank you, Agent Connelly," he said.

Meredeth signaled the waitress, and when the woman appeared, she ordered an English muffin and peanut butter.

After the waitress strolled back toward the kitchen, Roger lifted his gaze and met McCloe's direct gaze. "I've never told you why I joined the department. I understand why you may be suspicious in light of my absence, but if you knew why I'm a cop, you'd understand why I can't also be a serial killer." He glanced at Meredeth. "You'll understand why I don't match your generic profile, after all."

She nodded once and twirled her index finger.

"Right," he said. "When I was little—maybe between the ages of three and five—my mother had to work a couple of jobs. A couple, heh." He looked anything but amused. "She worked two full-time jobs and a part-time one on the weekends. Around the holidays, she'd pick up a fourth, doing seasonal stuff at the mall after her day jobs during the week. Sometimes she worked thirty-six hours without coming home. She worked herself to the bone for us."

"Us?" asked Cliff. "I thought you were an only child?"

"I was after the age of five." He cut his gaze to Meredeth's. "My brother was older than me—twelve years older. During that time when my mother was struggling to provide for us, Ralphie had to take care of me. He was fifteen when it started, and seventeen the day he died, but he never once complained—in my presence anyway. It meant he had to give up football. He had to quit school, you see, and created his own homeschool curriculum that he did when Mom was home or when I was asleep."

"That sounds rough, but—"

"Let me finish, Van Zandt. It'll make sense, I promise." He turned his gaze back on Meredeth but didn't quite meet hers this time. He appeared to be focused on her cheekbones. "One day, Ralphie put me down for a nap, and once I was asleep, he ran out to the market. I was out of my favorite snack and was grumpy about it." He fell silent as the waitress approached with Meredeth's new breakfast.

Once the waitress left, Meredeth picked up one side of her English muffin and spread butter first, then peanut butter across its surface. "Go on, Roger," she said. She picked up the other half and covered it with butter, then cherry preserves.

Roger dropped his gaze to his plate. "Some boys from his old high school—gang bangers who'd failed out for the year—accosted him on his way to the store. Ralph was a big kid. Six foot four at seventeen and weighed two hundred forty pounds. He didn't back down, and when they decided to mug him, he fought back. He broke one of the boy's arms and gave another a concussion. That's how we found out what happened—the boy with the broken arm went to the hospital, and the LASD matched hair and blood found at the scene to his. He rolled on his pals in exchange for a reduced sentence."

"That's rough," said Cliff.

Without lifting his gaze from the plate of rye toast, Roger nodded. "It destroyed my mom. I missed him, but I was too young to realize he'd *never* come home. Not for a few years, anyway." He fell silent and rubbed his eyes with his thumb and forefinger. "The guy rolled on his friends, like I said, and the cops caught the one with the concussion, but the ringleader got away clean. They had his name and his address, but his parents had sent him away the afternoon they killed Ralph." He shrugged. "There were rumors, of course. He was in south L.A. County. He was in Humboldt County. He went to St. Louis. Like that."

"And they never caught him, did they?" asked Meredeth.

He glanced at her and nodded once. "He's a fugitive to this day—if he's still alive. That was another rumor, that his older brother killed him in the bathtub for bringing the heat down on the family. Of course, that's just silly."

"And you joined LASD to find him?" asked Cliff.

Roger shook his head. "It would be great if I could, but I haven't looked for him. No, I joined the Sheriff's Department as a penance. Ralphie was only out that afternoon because I was being a brat, and he wanted me to chill out."

"No," said Meredeth. "His death wasn't your fault. You have nothing to pay penance for, Roger."

He shrugged. "Yes, I do. I have a lot to pay for, but not these murders." He treated her to an earnest gaze. "I became a cop to do my part in abolishing murder in L.A. County. I feel guilty about Ralphie's death as if I did it myself, but I've never committed a murder."

Interesting, Meredeth thought, *that he didn't say he's never killed anyone.* She glanced at Bobby, and his expression told her they were on the same wavelength.

"I know what it's like to have a family member murdered. I could never do that."

"I also have more experience with it than I'd like," said Meredeth. "Except it was my mother who was murdered, and it was my father who did it."

Roger's face twisted—as close to a compassionate grimace as he could get, it seemed. "Then you know."

"I'm not sure I do," said Meredeth. "I've certainly been tempted a time or two, and I have had to kill in the line of duty. Mister Sandman in Daytona Beach, Florida."

Roger nodded. "But that's not murder. 'In the line of duty' means you were protecting yourself or others. That's—"

"It's still taking a life," said Meredeth, softly. "It's still taking someone's brother or son off the face of the planet."

Roger took a bite of rye and chewed it methodically. "Can you imagine killing someone and *enjoying* it the way the unsub appears to?"

"No," she said and took a big peanut buttery bite of her English muffin.

Roger turned to Cliff. "Can you really imagine me doing those things to those women?"

"Not really," McCloe said matter-of-factly. "But if you were a good enough serial killer to pull this off for the fifteen years you've been a cop, you could make me think anything you wanted to."

"Maybe, maybe not. You're a good cop, Cliff. You have good instincts—better than mine." He shifted his gaze to Meredeth's. "And I don't think I could get anything past Agent Connelly."

"You might be surprised," said Meredeth. "I've been fooled before."

"Like I said: maybe I could, maybe not. I tend to think you'd see right through me if this morning is any indication of your skills." He turned his head to stare at the center of the table. "This is hard for me. I have a condition that makes reading people difficult for me in a context such as this. I don't know what any of you are thinking. I don't know if you're just humoring me."

"I'm not," said Cliff.

"In the end, Roger, it doesn't matter. We have to clear you, either way."

Roger's shoulders shot up and down in an eye blink. "Sure, I just don't know how. I was alone."

"We'll figure it out," said Cliff. "And the first thing we'll do is check in at Kindred Haven. Can we all agree that if Rog is on camera, we can rule him out?"

"Only if the timestamp is during the time when we had eyes on the unsub," said Bobby. "If it was after..."

"If it was after, we'll turn our attention to different methods," said Meredeth. "Traffic cams, GPS data from his Mazda."

"Thanks," Roger said. He pushed the plate of eggs away untouched and picked up a second triangle of rye toast. "I hate eggs."

CHAPTER 29

PHOTOGENIC

Sherman Oaks, CA

KINDRED HAVEN'S SECURITY office was a twelve-by-twelve windowless room in the hospital's basement. It was hot due to poor ventilation and the laundry that also resided in the basement. Two walls of the room were covered in flat-screen monitors from the top of the L-shaped desk to the ceiling. Two security officers sat watching the monitors, one facing south, the other west. The shift supervisor stood beside Meredeth, a remote in his hand, a keyboard resting on the end of the table in front of him. "This morning?"

"That's right," said Bobby. "Between half-past five and seven."

"It might take a while," said the supervisor. "That's a wide window."

"We understand," said Meredeth. "It's important and directly relevant to our investigation."

"Okay. Leave your number with me, and I'll—"

"We'll wait," said Roger in an iron tone.

"Suit yourself." The shift supervisor took over one of the monitors on the wall and pointed at it. "Watch here." He typed a query into the security software and waited a moment for the correct camera's footage to queue up. When an image appeared on the screen, he picked up the remote. "We'll watch it fast, so sing out if you see anything interesting."

"Go ahead," said Bobby.

With a nod, the supervisor tapped the fast-forward button a few times. "That's sixteen-x speed. If we don't see anything, we can try again on eight-x, then four, then two, then real-time. Hopefully, it won't come to that."

They watched the screen, the people flickering in and out of frame. The camera was one that focused on the front door of the lobby, and judging from the angle, Meredeth thought it must be directly over the information desk, though she didn't remember seeing one. Six minutes later, the supervisor sighed and turned to Roger. "Are you sure this is the right camera?"

"If those are the lobby entrance doors leading to Ventura, yes."

"The problem with these digital systems is that when you do a fast-forward, they jump forward in frames, so you don't actually see anything other than the original frame and then another sixteen frames ahead. That's why I suggested the tiered approach." He backed the footage up to the half-past-five mark and set the machine to replay the footage at eight times normal speed.

Meredeth tried to focus on the screen, but her head had gone into full power mode on the ride over from the diner. She had a giant, blurry C distorting everything she saw on the right side, and the pain in that eye throbbed with every beat of her heart. "Excuse me a moment," she said. "But don't stop the replay."

She turned and exited the small, overcrowded room. She found a public bathroom on the first floor and took the handicapped stall. She dropped her purse in the sink, then dug into the center pocket. She pulled out her pre-filled medicine container and grimaced. She'd forgotten her meds.

"I hope this works," she murmured. She flipped the lid of the day's container open and shook the pills into the palm of her left hand, then threw them toward the back of her mouth, transporting water to mouth with her cupped right hand. She swallowed the pills and grimaced at herself in the mirror as a massive bolt of pain lanced through her skull. "That's what you get for getting sloppy."

She left the restroom and walked across the lobby to the hospital gift shop for a can of Pepsi or Coke. But the gift shop carried bottles of iced coffee, and she took one of those, instead. After she paid the attendant, she retraced her steps to the basement and then to the security office. She opened the door quietly and slipped into the room.

"There!" said Roger in a victorious tone. "That's me, the one going out."

She glanced at the timestamp on the now frozen monitor—six thirty-nine, it read. *Not much help there*, she thought, then asked, "So that's when you left to head over to the courthouse, Roger?"

"Yeah," he said without taking his eyes off the screen. "There should be footage of me coming inside twenty or thirty minutes before this frame."

With a grunt, the senior security officer typed on the keyboard and the scene jumped to the lobby. He played the footage at real-time speed, and they all watched, each of them almost holding their breath. After four minutes and twenty-one seconds, snow rolled up from the bottom of the screen, obscuring the entire picture for just under three minutes.

"What was that?" asked Roger. "Where's the picture?"

"The stream might have gotten corrupted," said the security chief. "It happens with these high-camera-count digital systems from time to time." He continued the footage after the snow disappeared, but despite watching to the end, Roger did not appear in the footage.

"Let's go back to the snowy images," said Meredeth. "Say thirty minutes before. Then let's go frame by frame for a while to see if any imagery survived."

With a nod, the supervisor did as she asked, and again, they all watched in silence as frame after frame of snow showed on the screen. He kept pressing the frame advance button until the snow disintegrated from the bottom of the screen upward. When there was no more snow visible, he stopped pressing the button. "Sorry," he said. "But it looks like data loss to me."

"Maybe you can send that segment to this address?" Meredeth pulled out her business card and passed it over. "I'll send it to the Bureau's tech team."

"Happy to. I hope they can recover the data."

"Who's that?" asked Bobby. He was staring at the screen, where the frame remained frozen on a picture of a nearly deserted lobby. A man stood near the elevator, his head turned away. Another, older man, stood at the information desk with his back to the camera, reading something.

"Who's who?" asked Cliff. "And no, I'm not an owl. The guy at the desk?"

"Can you blow that image up?" asked Bobby. "Focus on the guy by the elevator."

Meredeth peered at the image, but the distance, the small screen, and her ever-present blurry C made it an exercise in futility.

"Sure can," said the security officer. He blew the image up with a few keystrokes, then moved over to the desk proper and used a mouse to center the screen on the guy. "Dark hair, maybe six feet tall."

"Can you advance the frame without losing the magnification?" asked Roger. "I remember the old man. He was grumbling about the visiting hours when I went by him."

"Was that before or after this?"

Roger shook his head. "I'm not sure, but I remember him"—he pointed at the old man—"but not him." He shifted his hand to point at the other man. "Maybe a few minutes before this."

"Are your cameras hard wired?" asked Bobby.

"No, Wi-Fi."

"What are you thinking, Bobby?"

He shrugged one shoulder and looked at her. "On one of my last...uh, trips over there, I had a...an assignment. Well, my team and I did. We were to..." He blew out a breath and glanced at the security officer. "There was a...house where someone was staying. Our orders were to, uh, get inside the house and secure the person. Easy enough, but there were cameras everywhere, and they were monitored by this guy's, um, crew, twenty-four seven. There was no real window for the op, so we went in at oh-dark-thirty via chopper. Anyway, the cameras were Wi-Fi and one of the SEALs had this gadget. Big red button on it. When he pressed the button, he ran straight past a camera, then turned and waved us in."

"And what was the big red button connected to?" asked Meredeth.

"He said it would interfere with the camera and make it blind until he turned it off. He said it was a Wi-Fi jammer."

Meredeth snapped her gaze back to the monitor. "Run it forward. Let's see if he ever faces the camera."

"No need," said the security supervisor. "That's Dr. Gull, the Chief of Surgery."

"Is it now?" asked Meredeth in a low voice.

"Why would he be trying to hide his face from the camera?"

The security guy ran forward a handful of frames—until Dr. Gull got on the elevator without ever turning his face back toward the camera. "Maybe the sun?"

"Those windows face south and a little west. Where would the sunlight be coming from?" asked Bobby.

The security officer only shook his head. "Listen..." He glanced at his underlings, then turned his back on them and stepped closer to Meredeth and Bobby. "You didn't hear me say this, okay?"

"Sure," said Meredeth.

"I mean, I don't know if you've ever worked in a hospital, but the doctors are like kings here. If one of them decides you're no good, you're out on your butt by the end of the day."

"We won't say anything," said Bobby.

The security supervisor looked Bobby in the eye, then nodded. "Okay. Dr. Gull is...a little bit out there if you know what I mean."

"Not really, no," said Meredeth.

The officer grimaced. "He's on his own wavelength. He comes across like he doesn't know us bugs exist. Oh, he can dance to the organ grinder's song when it's important. You know, turn on the charm, but you get the feeling his personality during those moments isn't real. Like he's acting. His real personality is the guy in that image, who turns away from the people in the lobby so no one can ask him a question. If that old man had left the desk and walked toward him, Dr. Gull would have walked away from the elevators. He'd have taken the stairs or the OR elevator. He *hates* talking to people unless he's getting something out of it."

Meredeth nodded. "I've heard him described as a real M. Deity."

"To be sure," said the supervisor, nodding emphatically. "But it's more than just that. I've had to talk to him one on one, and the whole conversation he stared at me with eyes that seemed dead, and I got the distinct feeling he wanted me to get out of his office despite the severity of the problem we were facing."

"Then this"—Meredeth gestured at the screen—"is pretty normal behavior for the man?"

"Well, I'm not sure the word normal applies to Dr. Gull, but had I seen this live, I wouldn't have raised an eyebrow."

"Thank you for your time. Please remember to email that file to me."

"I'll do it right away," he said. "Can you find your way back to the lobby, or should I go with you?"

"We'll be fine," said Meredeth.

CHAPTER 30

TALKING TO GOD

Sherman Oaks, CA

MEREDETH, BOBBY, AND the two LASD detectives stepped out into the hall, and Bobby pulled the security room door closed. Roger kept his eyes down, looking at his feet or the highly polished floor. "Maybe we should go talk to the good doctor," said Bobby. "Take him by surprise, put him off balance, and keep him teetering. Wi-Fi jammers are illegal. That should be enough to rattle his cage."

"But we don't know he was the one who used the jammer. Hell, we don't even know a jammer was used at all," said Cliff.

"True, but Gull doesn't know that," said Meredeth. She closed her eyes a moment—either the stress of the accelerating case or forgetting to take her meds had unleashed a monster head crusher.

"Are you..." Cliff raised his hands. "Can you do it? The interview, I mean."

"I can *always* do my job," Meredeth said with an acidic edge to her voice.

"I just meant—"

"No, I know," said Meredeth. "You'll have to forgive me until the Excedrin starts working."

"Okay," said Cliff. "What I meant was, are you feeling good enough to do an interview like you did in Volusia County?"

"Yes. Probably..." She closed her eyes again. "Maybe not. That was one of the best interviews I ever did. I don't know if I'll ever match that performance. But with you guys helping out..."

"You can count on it," said Roger. "I'd like to know if he was the one with the jammer. I'd like to know why he felt the need to use such a device that morning—or does he always do it? Some kind of paranoid compulsion?"

"No idea," said Meredeth. "But let's get to it."

They traipsed back to the elevators and rode one to the fifth floor, then strolled back to Aaron Gull's office door. Meredeth nodded, and Bobby knocked, then tried to open the door immediately but found it locked. "Dr. Gull?" he called through the door. "It's Bobby Van Zandt from the FBI. We have a couple more questions for you." He waited about thirty seconds, then knocked on the door again, harder and with more authority. "Dr. Gull?" That time, he was rewarded with noise from within the office.

"What?" shouted Dr. Gull. "I said don't disturb me until my ten o'clock surgery!"

"Dr. Gull, it's Special Agent Van Zandt from the Federal Bureau of—"

The door sprang open, and Gull stood in the doorway, eyes bloodshot, sleep nesting in the corners of his eyes, his clothes disheveled and wrinkled. "Can you come back later? I need time to prepare for my surgery."

"This won't take long. We have a few follow-up questions."

"But I already told you everything I know," he said in a tone that was almost that of a whiny teenager.

"That's okay," said Meredeth. "Look, the reality is, we need to ask you about your Wi-Fi jammer."

Gull's eyes snapped to hers, and his lips thinned into a white line. "My *what?*"

"Come on, Doc," said Bobby. "We've just come from reviewing the security footage from this morning. We saw you jam the Wi-Fi for the lobby cameras. We just need to know why."

With narrowed eyes, Gull examined each of them in turn, starting with Meredeth, then the LASD detectives, then ending with Bobby. "You're mistaken." His voice was firm, confident. "I don't even know what a Wi-Fi jammer is."

Meredeth inclined her head. "Dr. Gull, we're hunting a serial killer. We don't care about your little toy, and as long as you promise to get rid of it, we don't need to arrest you or even refer you to the FCC."

He turned to her, a furrow-line appearing between his brows. "Why would you..." He shook his head. "Never mind."

"Can we come in?" she asked. "I've got a boomer of a headache, and I'd like to sit down a moment."

Gull's face went slack a moment, and his eyes transformed into lifeless dark orbs like doll's eyes. He stepped back and grunted, then turned and disappeared within.

With a glance at Bobby, Meredeth stepped in after him and walked over to one of his visitor chairs and sank into its comfortable embrace. Gull was already seated across the broad oak plane of his fancy desk.

"You understand, if a doctor were to use a Wi-Fi jammer on the lobby cameras, his action would be self-defense."

"From what?" asked Cliff as he came into the office and leaned against the windowsill.

"Those security people. They enjoy recording doctors coming in off-hours and posting them on social media. You know, 'look at the sleepy doctor with his shirt tail stuck in his zipper.' It's tiresome."

"I see. Were you aware the devices are illegal?"

"No. At least, not in so many words. I knew they were gray at best, though. But tell me, Agent Connelly, is it really okay to have your worst moments captured by your workplace security system and then posted to Instagram or TikTok or whatever the new thing is?"

Meredeth shook her head. "Cliff or Roger, want to take that one?"

Roger nodded. "Dr. Gull, the actions you've described are likely problematic. It's true that the lobby isn't a prohibited or private space where video may not be employed, but taking the video from the hospital and posting it publicly... No, any sane judge would rule that an invasion of privacy, especially as this is a hospital, and any video you show up in may also include patients."

"And security systems may only be used as such—for security," said Cliff.

"Then you see?" said Gull. "Our security department doesn't find an issue with posting embarrassing videos online. It might be that several doctors got together and found a solution, then told every other physician who practices here."

"And that physician might be a chief of a department," said Meredeth drolly.

Gull nodded slowly, his gaze burning on her own.

"Well, I guess that clears it up," said Bobby, and he, Cliff, and Roger got to their feet.

"Then if you'll please allow me to get back to my meditations, I—"

"I guess there's one more thing," said Meredeth.

"Oh?"

Meredeth nodded. "The reason we were viewing the security footage is that we believe the man who killed Mary Ann Blocker killed again early this morning. We have witness statements that place the man in the lobby downstairs around half-past six, but your little jammer blocked that footage. Did you happen to see a man in black ahead of you in the lobby?"

"No. There was an old man muttering to himself at the info desk, but that's the only person I saw."

"How about after you? For example, as you stepped into the elevator, did you notice anyone entering the lobby?"

"Sorry," Gull said, "I simply can't help you."

"Well, drat," said Meredeth, putting on one of her blinding smiles.

"Then—"

"Just one last question. If your surgery isn't until later this morning, why did you come in before seven?"

"What? I..." He dropped his gaze to his desktop blotter. "That is, I like to come in early before a big surgery. I like to lock myself away in my office and spend a few hours alone."

"Meditating," said Bobby.

"Yes. Visualization is a very powerful tool for a surgeon. I run through the steps and actions I will take in the upcoming surgery, visualizing my success. I do that several times, and for longer surgeries like the one I will perform later this morning, that takes time. I also practice complications, and how I will react to them."

"Wow," said Cliff. "There's a lot more to being a surgeon than installing zippers."

Gull looked at him and bunched his brows. He opened his mouth to speak, but Cliff held up his hand. "I used to do stand-up. Sometimes the urge for a zinger is too strong to resist. I apologize."

"Very well," said Gull. He turned an inquisitive gaze on Meredeth.

"Oh! Sorry." She rose and walked toward the door. "Thanks for clearing all this up for us, Dr. Gull."

"Yes. Please close the door on your way out."

With a nod, Meredeth stepped through the door, followed by the three investigators with her, and Bobby pulled the door to. He put his finger to his lips and leaned his head close to the door. After a moment, he was rewarded with the sound of Gull locking the door. They walked away, then stopped in the surgical waiting room.

"Now what?" asked Cliff.

"I want to verify his story. I think Mildred McFadden can do that for us. I'll go call her down." She left the waiting room and headed down the hall to the yellow phone hanging on the wall.

She picked up the phone and waited through the soft beeps until someone picked up. "Hello, this is Special Agent Meredeth Connelly. Is this Mildred?"

"No, she's got the day off."

"Oh, okay. I'll give her a call on her cell phone." She hung up the yellow phone, pinched the bridge of her nose, then fished out her Excedrin and dry swallowed another dose. With that done, she turned around and went to get the others.

CHAPTER 31

ROLL CALL

Sherman Oaks, CA

MEREDETH'S PHONE RANG as she stepped through the glass doors onto the sidewalk. She glanced down at the caller ID, then at Bobby. "I need to take this," she said to Cliff. "I'll meet you all at the car."

Bobby sidled close to her. "Kevin?" he asked sotto voce.

She gave him a curt nod, then lifted the phone to her ear as Bobby walked fast to catch up to the two detectives. "Good morning, Kevin," she said after accepting his call.

"It's early enough for roll call, but I figured you'd be up and at 'em."

"Indeed. There was another murder last night."

"Oh, no. You're sure it's the same guy?"

"Absolutely, he left another quote from the 'Little Whores' poem. But he customized it for me. Want to hear it?"

"Why not?"

"'Connelly may save one, then there'll be seven. Seven little whores, all far too willing. This one stays here, there's been a killing.' Then he wrote, 'Catch me if you can, Connelly' beneath it. Sweet, huh?"

"That's not the word I'd choose. Your unsub knows you're in town, knows you're working the case. Are you taking precautions?"

"Kev, I always take precautions. The Alex thing was a fluke. I mean, women serial killers are rare enough to discount the idea in almost every case, but transgender serial killers are even farther afield."

"I know the statistics, but I don't care. I care that you come home under your own power without any new scars."

"I know. I'm being careful, and I've got Bobby."

"Do I have to call him and put him on Meredeth-watch?"

"If you do, you'd better run when you see me next."

"I may do that anyway. Cooties."

"I'll give you cooties, right in the chops."

"Sounds kinky. Do you have any good suspects yet?"

"Maybe. One of the detectives was A.W.O.L. during the second crime scene investigation. He fits the profile on every point, I think. We're trying to rule him out but ran into technical difficulties caused by the second suspect."

"Are they in cahoots?"

"No. Neither one of them could have a partner, I think. Dr. Gull is as strange or stranger than Roger. He actually uses a Wi-Fi jammer to take out the security cameras as he enters the hospital."

"Well, that's illegal."

"Yeah. We may use that later to get him in the box if he stops cooperating with my questions. He claims he runs the jammer because the security folks post videos of the doctors looking like crap coming in off-hours."

"I guess I understand that. Who wants extra fuel for a malpractice suit?"

"I'm not sure I believe him."

"That generally means you don't believe him but don't know why."

"Isn't it great we know each other so well?"

"It is," he said solemnly. "Now, tell me about the cop. What's his name?"

"Roger Shelton. He's a strange egg, very opinionated, very stand-offish. There's what he did at dinnertime last night. He was unreachable all morning until he decided to call Cliff. We went to breakfast and on the way, we told him he was a perfect match for the initial profile. He refused to come inside and eat with us, but later, he did just that. He says he can't be the killer because his older brother and caregiver was mugged and killed by a couple of gang bangers, and he decided to be a cop to do his part in reducing the murder rate."

"Hmm. Doesn't sound like a get out of jail free card."

"No, but he did sound sincere."

"Have you changed your mind about him?"

"No. We went back to the hospital to check the security footage, hoping we could rule him out by his presence there, but we only have an image of him leaving the hospital. That's how we discovered Gull's little trick, but that occurred twenty minutes or so before Roger's departure. That wouldn't rule him out, because everything was over by then."

"Ah."

"Bobby spotted the unsub watching us from a nearby building's roof. He almost nabbed the guy, but the unsub made it to his getaway car, then eluded everyone. Not even a civilian spotted his car."

"That's too bad. No plates, I guess?"

"No, it was dark, and Bobby was in search and destroy mode, though he didn't take a shot because of the houses in the backdrop."

"Smart, then."

"Yeah."

"Meredeth, you brought up Alex a minute ago. I'm not comfortable with another potential situation where someone on your team might turn against you during a gunfight. Can't you request his removal from the investigation?"

"No, I don't think we're there yet."

"You *are* there, though. You already can't trust the guy. Do you want him behind you in CQB?"

"Look at you with your fancy acronyms."

"I'm serious, FBI."

"Yeah, I know, HRT."

"Bobby can't guard you against unseen threats *and* this Shelton guy."

"Probably not, Kev, but I'm not defenseless. I'm not some lacquered-nails girlie-girl who needs a big man to protect me."

"I didn't mean to imply you were, but let's face it, Mere. Even you must admit you get a little target-fixated from time to time."

"Yes, that's true. That's how Alex got me from behind. I was too focused on the idea of a male killer. All Alex had to do was report a sighting of a man watching us. Then again, he was all dressed up as Sonya Sargent."

"Right. I'm not saying you should have spotted that coming. What I'm saying is, you're in the exact same predicament, but this time, you have reason to suspect Roger. Good reason. I'm sure if you spoke to the Homicide Division commander, he'd see your point."

"I'm not comfortable putting a mark on his record at this point."

"Forget his record, Mere. Let's focus on you keeping all your insides beneath your skin."

"I am, Kevin. I always do. And there's Bobby. Hey, you know I think he might have been in on the raid of Osama bin Laden's house. He told a story with details that matched some of what happened in that raid. That's how we knew about the Wi-Fi jammer. A SEAL on the raid had one to zap the defenses of the compound. I found it—"

"No offense to Bobby, Mere, but at this moment, I'm not interested in the story. I'm—"

"Kevin, I know. Can we move on?"

"It's hard for me to move on when you've got your head in the sand."

"But I don't, Kevin. I'm being careful around Roger. We all are. I'll never be alone with him."

"I suppose that will have to do."

"Then you'll drop this?"

"Sure," he lied.

CHAPTER 32

THE HOUSEMAID

South of Santa Clara, CA

MILDRED MCFADDEN'S ADDRESS was a giant thing on top of the hills outside Santa Clara. It was almost forty-five minutes away via I-5, and the ride to her house was full of fluff talk and uncomfortable silences. Roger kept to himself, mostly, and the rest of them were content to let him, but as they pulled into the cobblestone drive, he sat up straight and peered around as if looking for something.

Cliff parked in the semi-circle drive in front of the larger double doors and whistled. "Must be rough having to camp out."

"Yeah," said Bobby. "How many square feet is that monstrosity?"

Roger tilted his head to the side. "I'd say seventy-five hundred to eight thousand."

"I'd hate to have to clean that place," said Meredeth as she got out. She walked to the front door and pressed the bell.

After a few minutes, a woman in her late twenties opened the door. "Yes?"

"I'm Special Agent Meredeth Connelly. I'm here to speak with Mrs. McFadden."

"I'm afraid Mildred doesn't see anyone without an appointment."

"It's okay, Freida, let the FBI in." Mildred's voice came from somewhere to the right and sounded exhausted to the point of collapse.

Meredeth smiled at Freida. "Would you like to see my credentials?"

The young woman gave her a look, then switched her gaze to the three men behind Meredeth.

"My partner, Special Agent Van Zandt, Detective McCloe, and Detective Shelton, both of the LASD."

Freida shrugged and stepped back from the door, beckoning them inside. "Millie is in the study," she said. She raised her left arm and pointed to a smaller set of double doors to the right of the atrium.

"Thank you, Freida," said Meredeth. She turned toward the study, crossed the marble slab flooring, and knocked on the doors.

"Come in, Meredeth," croaked Mildred from within.

Meredeth opened the rightmost door and stepped through it. The room was grand indeed, lined with built-in cherry bookshelves and cabinets on every wall. The marble slab floor continued into the room, though a large area rug covered the center. On the rug were a desk and several comfortable armchairs that had been crowded to the side to make room for the infusion chair that faced an enormous bay window that filled the room with sunlight. To her left was a bucket—thankfully, empty.

Mildred McFadden sat in the infusion chair hooked up to an IV that contained something translucent and chartreuse at the same time. "Come in and make yourselves comfortable." Next to her within easy reach, was a folding table that held a laptop, an open book lying face down, an enormous pitcher of what appeared to be lemonade, a half-full glass of the same, and a telephone. Mildred took a deep breath and let it out slowly, her eyes closed.

Meredeth pulled one of the armchairs over, and her cadre followed suit. She sat across from Mildred. "Chemo?" she asked in a quiet voice.

Mildred nodded. "Every four days, and between the infusions I have to do leucovorin rescues to keep the cure from killing me dead." She sounded horrible—beyond exhausted, beyond sick.

"That looks too evil to be a cure," said Bobby.

"Methotrexate. High dose, which is why it would kill me without the leucovorin."

"Leukemia?" asked Roger without looking at her.

"No, primary CNS Lymphoma. This is my second relapse. I also do radiation treatments at the hospital."

"I wish you the best," said Meredeth. "It must be tough to carry on working." She looked around. "Especially if you don't have to."

Mildred laughed weakly. "Oh, I do. Otherwise, I'd be home all the time with my husband, Daniel." She grimaced and closed her eyes again.

"We don't have to do this now," said Meredeth. "We can come back later—even tomorrow."

"No, no," said McFadden. "I'm an old hand at this. Live every day, no matter how you may feel. Go ahead with your questions, I'm glad of the company."

"If you're sure," said Meredeth.

"I am."

"We spoke with Dr. Gull this morning, and we'd like to confirm a few things about his schedule and his practices."

"His scheduling changes from day to day, but I can help you with the latter part."

"Okay. He told us that when he has an early morning surgery, he likes to come in several hours early and meditate on the upcoming techniques he'll need, including what he will do in the face of complications. Does that jive with your experiences with him?"

"Yes. He does that frequently. Sometimes he comes in during the early morning hours—even three in the morning if the surgery is scheduled in the first slot."

"I see," said Meredeth. "And how often would you say he does this?"

"On routine surgeries, he doesn't bother, but on big or complicated surgeries, he always does." She tilted her head back and gazed at the ceiling. "Well, perhaps 'always' is too aggressive a word. Let's just say I don't have any memories of him not coming in early for the types of surgeries I mentioned."

"Thank you," said Meredeth. "We're sorry to have disturbed you."

Mildred chuckled weakly. "Disturb me, please. Save me from these interminable infusions."

Meredeth scooted forward to the edge of her chair, making ready to stand, but then she stopped and looked Mildred in the eye. "He's a strange one, Dr. Gull, isn't he?"

McFadden's face went through a series of permutations on a theme—discomfort. "I don't like to speak poorly about a person."

"Then you agree?"

"Most physicians are a bit different, but especially the type driven to achieve as Dr. Gull is. Did you know he's the youngest chief of surgery Kindred Haven has ever had? And a lot of the nurses tend to see him as a crusty slavedriver, but they don't realize he drives himself harder than he drives anyone else. He demands perfection of himself and expects no less than anyone else."

"Would you be comfortable in a private meeting with him? One in which there was no one around but the two of you?" asked Cliff.

"I am a married woman," said Mildred.

"That's not really an answer," murmured Roger.

Mildred glanced at him and frowned. "No, I suppose it isn't."

"Pretend you weren't married. If he asked you to come to his place for dinner, would you go?" asked Cliff.

"Well..." Mildred closed her eyes and breathed through her slightly parted lips. "Just a moment."

"We're sorry to have bothered you," said Meredeth. "You don't have to answer."

"No, no. I don't think I would accept his invitation. He's a good-looking man, but I'm afraid I've seen all sides of Dr. Gull, and I don't like some of those sides."

"Would you feel safe alone with him?" asked Meredeth. "Say there was some issue that required the two of you to be in the surgery suite alone."

Mildred opened her eyes and shook her head. "That, I wouldn't enjoy."

"Why?" asked Cliff.

"Because... Because sometimes he looks at a nurse he's not happy with, and his eyes...they make you want to run and hide."

"Anger? Rage?"

Mildred shook her head. "No. He might be screaming at the poor nurse, but his eyes are cold. He looks at them without any sign of human regard or compassion."

"Well, thank you for answering our questions," Meredeth said, rising. "I'll keep you and your cancer in my thoughts."

"Thank you, Agent Connelly." She reached for her phone. "Let me call Freida to come see you to the door."

"It's no bother," said Meredeth. "We remember the way."

"As you wish," said Millie.

They tromped out to the car, and Cliff got them back onto I-5. "Well, where to?"

"Let's take a trip to the ME's office," said Meredeth. "I'd like to get those postmortems ASAP."

Cliff shrugged and switched to the fast lane.

What little conversation there was as the miles ticked by died when his cell phone rang. He had it connected through the Impala's system via Bluetooth and accepted the call by pressing a button on the steering wheel. "McCloe," he said.

"McCloe, this is Chief Marcus."

"Yes, Chief."

"Am I on speakerphone?"

"Yes, sir. I'm driving on the 5, headed toward the ME."

"And are our FBI friends with you?"

"Yes."

"Shelton, as well?"

"Yes, sir, he's right here."

"Fine, fine. Drop the ME trip and meet me at the West Hollywood Station. I'm there now."

"Yes, sir," said Cliff. "It may be a while."

"That's okay, McCloe. This is important."

"Yes, sir."

"See you soon."

"Yes, sir." The chief disconnected, and Cliff glanced at Roger. "I wonder what that's all about."

Roger shrugged and looked out the passenger side window.

"I hope there's been a break in the case and we're meeting an assault team," said Cliff. "I'd love to put all this behind us."

CHAPTER 33

ON THE CARPET

West Hollywood, CA

THE RED BRICK station house was one of those angular affairs with a stepped roof. The interior had that police station smell—black coffee, body odor, gun oil, and cologne. Lots of cologne. Meredeth and Bobby followed Cliff and Roger as they navigated the hallways and threaded through bullpens for patrol and the West Hollywood detectives.

Chief Marcus stepped out of the station captain's office and beckoned them. "McCloe and Shelton, inside."

Meredeth and Bobby slowed, then changed directions for the breakroom.

"Agents Connelly and Van Zandt, don't go far. I want to talk to you next."

"Yes, sir," said Bobby as he pointed at the break room.

Chief Marcus nodded, then turned and went into the office.

"I wonder what all this is about," murmured Bobby.

"Got me. Something internal, maybe."

"Did you..." Bobby shook his head. "Nah, never mind."

"Come on, Bobby," she said, massaging her temples. "Don't make me pull the question out of you."

"Fine," he said with a shrug. "Did you communicate our suspicions about Roger to McCutchins?"

She shook her head. "No."

Bobby relaxed a skosh. "Good."

Meredeth sat on the couch and leaned her head back against the wall. "Maybe they did find something and want to stage a raid."

"In your dreams."

"Yeah," she said and sighed.

Out in the hall, a door slammed, and a few moments later, Roger Shelton stormed past the breakroom. His head was down, but his complexion was red with strong emotion. He didn't look at them, didn't look at anyone, only stomped down the hall, and a few moments later, another door slammed hard.

"Uh oh," said Bobby. "I think the fit just hit the shan."

Meredeth frowned and bunched her brows. "The only person I told about our suspicions was Kevin."

"You don't think he called out here, do you?"

"No, Kevin wouldn't do that. Besides, he said he'd drop it as long as I promised to be careful."

"Ah," said Bobby in a non-committal tone.

"What?"

"Nothing."

"Bobby..."

In the hall, another door opened, but this time it closed quietly. Footsteps approached the break room, and Cliff stopped in the doorway, staring down the hall. After a moment, he turned and looked at them. "That was really uncalled for."

"What?" asked Meredeth. "We didn't do anything."

Cliff looked in the direction that Roger had gone. "You might have ruined his career."

"Cliff, we didn't do *anything.*"

He hooked his thumb over his shoulder. "Chief Marcus wants you two. I'm going to see if I can find Roger. Meet in the car when you're done in there."

"Really, Cliff, we didn't do anything. We didn't speak to anyone in your chain of command about our suspicions."

"Yeah." He walked away without another word.

Meredeth glanced at Bobby and twitched her shoulders up, then down. "I hope we're not getting blamed for—"

"Come on. Let's go find out what this is all about." He stood and headed toward the door. Meredeth got up and followed him.

Chief Marcus stood in the doorway of the station captain's office, his face a granite slab, his eyes smoldering. "Get in here," he said.

"Chief, what's going on?" Meredeth asked. "What's happened with Shelton?"

"As if you don't know." He turned and disappeared inside the office, leaving Meredeth and Bobby to follow.

As they entered the office, Marcus was rounding the desk. He sat in the chair and clasped his hands in front of him as though he worried he might do something he'd regret. "Sit," he ordered.

Meredeth and Bobby sat, sharing a glance as they did so.

"Now, one of you owes me an explanation."

"Chief," said Meredeth, "we're in the dark here. Can you please tell us what's going on?"

The chief rolled his eyes and shook his head once. "Shelton's out. You got what you wanted."

Meredeth held up her hands, palms toward the chief. "Wait a minute, Chief Marcus. We don't want animosity here. We are here to assist *your* department find this serial killer. The way I see it, cooperation is key. Cliff McCloe is a fine officer and—"

"But not Shelton, is that it?"

"I didn't say that," said Meredeth quietly. "Can you tell us why Roger stomped out of here like a spurned lover?"

"The sheriff got a call this morning. From some guy named McCutchins back at Quantico."

"Jim McCutchins is our boss," said Bobby.

"But we haven't spoken to him since he sent us out here," added Meredeth. "There's no reason to, at this point. We don't have anything solid on the unsub."

Chief Marcus sniffed and dropped his gaze to his blanching knuckles. "I don't suppose you know why McCutchins would call and request we take Roger Shelton off the case?" He raised his head and glared at Meredeth. "Why he would say it was for *your* safety?"

Meredeth closed her eyes. "Dammit, Kevin," she murmured.

"What was that?"

"My...my boyfriend. I spoke to him about the case—he's FBI, too, an instructor at the academy and an HRT member. I told him about our concerns, but I—"

"Concerns about Roger Shelton?"

"Yes, sir," said Bobby.

"And they are?"

"Well, Roger has displayed some strange behavior," said Meredeth. "And he was A.W.O.L. at this morning's crime scene. That set us all thinking, McCloe included. I have a preliminary profile of the unsub, and Roger ticks all the boxes. But we have no proof. In fact, we spent part of our morning trying to check his alibi."

"McCloe told me. Any word from the data analysis crew at Quantico?"

Meredeth shook her head. "Nothing yet."

"And do you believe Roger is the unsub?"

"I don't know," said Meredeth, "but it's possible."

Marcus shook his head. "Well, he's off the case as of now. He's riding a desk until we catch the bastard killing women in Sherman Oaks or until we can clear him. What's this profile?"

Meredeth leaned forward. "Chief, we"—she waved her hand at Bobby—"did not ask anyone to remove Roger."

"Fill me in on the profile."

"Okay. The unsub is a white male between the ages of thirty and fifty. He's got a job, likely with flexible hours. He's strong and rugged. He dresses well, but nothing that would stand out in a crowd, and nothing offensive. He's a loner and doesn't much care for the company of people or crowds. He's single and may be bashful around women he's sexually interested in. He's eccentric—odd, maybe— and stand-offish. He's irritable in the company of more than a few people or maybe in groups larger than one. He lives in or around Sherman Oaks and is very familiar with the area. He probably has a storage unit or warehouse space near Ventura Avenue—something large enough to hide a full-sized American car like the one that fled the scene this morning. He drives a dark-colored car, probably an SUV, but like his clothing, nothing flashy, nothing souped up or blinged out."

Marcus was quiet a moment, then he relaxed his grip. "That does sound like Shelton."

Meredeth shrugged uneasily. "And a lot of other people. We do have another suspect, as well."

"Then Roger is a suspect."

"We have to consider him until we can rule him out. That's just the way this works."

"Yeah," said the chief, then he sighed and leaned back in his chair, ignoring the squeak. "Roger should be riding a desk. He doesn't like it, but that's the way it has to be until he's cleared. He should get a rip for missing the call out this morning, too. We've always turned a blind eye to his eccentric behavior about coming in on time because he closes cases. But with something like this, it's better to exclude him from the suspect pool before we put him back in the field. If nothing else, so you can focus on the investigation. Your boss didn't want your attention split between what's in front of you *and* the detective standing behind you."

"He can be overprotective since I was stabbed six months ago."

"She almost died," said Bobby. "She was attacked by the Pass-a-Grille Killer, who was in disguise and functioning as a member of our team."

Chief Marcus glanced at her, and sympathy replaced the anger in his eyes. "I guess I can understand his insistence."

"Like I said, overprotective," said Meredeth. "Is Cliff still on the case?"

"Yes. He and Roger will remain partners until there's ample evidence suggesting that needs to change. I don't think I'll assign him a temporary partner since he's got the two of you."

"That's fine," said Bobby. "He's good."

"He is," said Chief Marcus. "Tell me how we can exclude Roger."

"As of now, the only way we have is by comparing his whereabouts during the time of the murder. He doesn't have much—just his assertion that he was at Kindred Haven Hospital, following up on something that he didn't share. It might be a good idea to have him surveilled when he's off shift. We can clear him if there's another murder and can prove Roger was in a different location."

"How about GPS from his phone?"

"He could leave it at home," said Meredeth. "He could give it to a friend and have them drive around in another part of L.A."

"What about a house arrest ankle bracelet? We'd know if he tampered with it, and in the meantime, it gives us a solid GPS every fifteen minutes."

Meredeth nodded. "That could work if he'll go along with it."

"He will," said Marcus in a firm voice.

"Then that will work."

"Good. Roger is too good a detective to waste on paperwork. The sooner we can either get him cleared or arrest him, the better."

CHAPTER 34

SAINT ANGER

Sherman Oaks, CA

DRUITT DROVE THE streets of Sherman Oaks the way he used to. He cruised the spots where prostitutes were known to hang out, looking for a petite beauty with dark hair and a sexy smile. Rage thrummed through him. His latest escapade hadn't given Connelly the least bit of pause, and his run-in with Van Zandt hadn't done much for his ego, either. And then there was the nonsense at work.

"How did he see me? I was *hidden* up there. It was night, for the love of Mike." There was no one to answer him, except the nagging voice in the back of his mind telling him to get out, to run before Connelly and Van Zandt locked him up. "Ridiculous," he grumbled.

He drove on, searching for the right woman, the right whore, the perfect match to advance his tribute to the enigmatic Jack the Ripper. He'd cheated a little to check Dark Annie off the list, and truth be told, the woman he'd picked up in the club wasn't as perfect for the role as she could have been.

There was always room to improve, and he aimed to do so. He needed someone tall to match Long Liz, or at least someone with an appropriate surname. He could fudge things a bit on first names due to the new time restraints he was functioning under, but Jack would spin in his grave if he used a short woman named Smith or something equally inane.

To make matters worse, he needed *two victims* in the next eighteen hours, and without preparation, that might be a tall order. *Oh, well*, he thought, *everyone has problems. I'll do my best, and my best is significantly better than others I can think of.*

All the self-talk had distracted him from his fury a little. He still felt the emotion roaring around, just under the surface of his thoughts, but he could *think* and *plan* again. Maybe he'd use Meredeth Connelly for the last in the series. "M" first name for Marie Jeanette. That could work. And Marie Jeanette's real name had been Mary Jane Kelly, an Irish last name, so Connelly could fit as well. He smiled a little, sure he looked like a maniac but not caring in the least.

The girls near Burbank and Sepulveda Boulevards were scarce, and the ones he could pick out as whores didn't meet his standards. They were fat, ugly, and obvious coke addicts, what have you.

He continued north, passing the hooker hotels that dotted Sepulveda like condom wrappers. Places with names like El Pizzaro and Cobertiza Hotel, but he saw no one out advertising her wares. *Maybe it's too early*, he thought. *No one has any work ethic anymore.* He continued past them and drove on. He had one last place to check: La Infidelidad, which was beyond the commercial area he was driving through and marked the beginning of the residential area.

"If there's no one suitable, I'll cruise south on Van Nuys Boulevard. I might spot someone there." There was more risk, especially when he neared the courthouse and LAPD station nearby, but he knew ways to get the job done without much risk, except if a police officer saw him.

He completed his tour of Sepulveda Boulevard and Van Nuys Boulevard, then turned left on Ventura. He couldn't deny he was disappointed, but his work was like fishing: sometimes he came back with nothing to show for his efforts. He drove east, toward his storage spot, frowning a little at his failure to find a Long Liz stand-in.

He passed the stupid hospital on his left. *What the hell kind of name is Kindred Haven, anyway?* He shook his head and adjusted the air conditioning a little. When he lifted his head, he saw her and smiled.

CHAPTER 35

THE SOUND OF SILENCE

Los Angeles, CA

CLIFF DIDN'T HAVE much to say to either of them when they caught up to him at the Impala. His expression was stony, his eyes cool and flinty. He motioned for someone to take the front passenger seat, and Meredeth could almost hear the recrimination in the gesture—*sit up front...might as well because Roger won't be needing it.*

She took the passenger seat, and Bobby climbed in the back. "Look, Cliff, we didn't put Roger in the hot seat. Our boss called the sheriff without speaking to us."

"Yeah? Well, here in California, we don't tell the suits about something like this until we know for sure."

Meredeth adjusted her seatbelt, and Cliff turned the ignition. "Well, we didn't either. We haven't even spoken to our boss since we arrived—nothing to report yet. But I did talk it over with my boyfriend. He just hired on to the FBI, though, and must have spoken to Jim about it. Since I was stabbed, he's a little nuts about my personal safety."

"Huh," said Cliff, and that was all he said, but the temperature seemed to rise a little from the subarctic freeze.

"I'm going to speak to him about it," said Meredeth. "He was state police in New York, then ran his own police department. He knows better than this. He knows how something like this hurts good cops."

"So now Roger's a good cop?" Cliff glanced at her, and she saw the anger in his eyes.

"You've said so," she said. "Personally, I have no idea, but I would have preferred to find out rather than just sideline him based on half-baked suspicion."

"I hope you told Chief Marcus that."

"I did, and I hope you'll pass the sentiment on to Roger."

"I will when I find him."

"I thought he was assigned to a desk?" asked Bobby.

Cliff gave a slow nod. "Yeah, but he wasn't there. A patrol officer told me he saw Roger storm out."

"Should we go look for him?"

"I don't think that would be wise. He's furious, and it takes him a while to calm down. It's best to leave him alone."

Meredeth shrugged. "Okay. Then let's head over to the ME's office. We might as well see what the cutters have to say."

"Ten-four," said Cliff.

The West Hollywood station house was on the corner of North San Vicente and Santa Monica, and the county medical examiner's office was on the corner of North Mission Road and Marengo Street—only sixteen miles apart but on the route the GPS on her phone suggested, it would take them one and a half hours.

"I didn't think anywhere could surpass D.C. traffic," said Meredeth. "But I think ninety minutes to travel sixteen miles might take the cake."

"Nah, nah," said Cliff. "You're riding with a native. We'll be there in half that time."

"That's more reasonable," said Bobby with the slight twang that meant he was being sarcastic. "Three minutes per mile."

"It's better than six minutes," said Cliff with a shrug. He drove surface roads until he hit I-10, then took that until he could jump on the 5 northbound. The first thing they saw upon entering the county complex was the visitors' entrance of the medical examiner's office—an old three-story building with a dramatic entrance and gold-leaf lettering on the windows. Cliff turned to the right and followed the road around to the modern concrete and glass building to the side of the historic building. He parked in one of the restricted spots and flipped down the visor placard that identified the Impala as a Sheriff's Department vehicle.

He led them inside and took them straight to the office of the coroner assigned to the case. Her name was Dr. Nina Winchester, a mid-forties bombshell with dark hair and eyes and buttery smooth olive-toned skin. "Hey, Nina," Cliff said. "This is Special Agent Meredeth Connelly and Special Agent Bobby Van Zandt."

Dr. Winchester nodded to them. "Where's Roger today? Off pouting?"

"You could say that," said Cliff.

She shrugged and turned to Meredeth. "Hi, I'm Nina." She extended a hand, which Meredeth shook.

"And I'm Meredeth. He's Bobby."

Nina winked at Bobby and shook his hand. "I wonder if I can get a job with the Bureau."

"Probably," Bobby said with a grin. "If you knew a guy."

"And do I?"

"Sure," he said, "but I don't know why you'd want to leave this great weather in exchange for snow, ice, and windstorms."

"Have you *seen* L.A.?" she asked with a laugh.

"Some of it," he said.

"Nina, we're here to check in on how you're doing with Mary Ann Blocker. It's too soon for this morning's victim, we understand that, but is there anything beyond what met the eye in Blocker's case?"

"The neck lacerations ran very deep. He almost severed her spine, the poor girl. Also, the abdominal stab wounds pierced her uterus and vagina. He also removed five of her teeth, and based on the CSI reports, he took them as souvenirs, leaving a slight laceration on her tongue. The tox report isn't back yet, but prelim blood work is all normal, except for a qualitative HCG. Based on her levels of HCG, I dissected her uterus. She was in the first trimester."

"Pregnant?" Cliff asked.

"Yes," said Meredeth. "That's potential motive, right there." She turned her attention back to Nina. "Did she show signs of fighting back?"

Nina nodded. "Her right knee is heavily bruised like you might expect from blocked groin shots. There were no defensive wounds on her hands, but being a nurse, I suspect she had both hands clamped across the neck wound to delay unconsciousness for as long as possible."

"She tried to get away," said Meredeth. "The blood spatter backs that up."

Nina nodded. "I'm sorry there's not much more."

"The pregnancy is new," said Meredeth.

"Boyfriend?" asked Nina.

Meredeth shook her head. "A string of one-night stands according to her best friend."

Nina shrugged. "I've done a prelim physical on the second vic. Her name was Catherine Endicott, twenty-four years old, residing in Van Nuys. Of course, there's no blood work or anything, but based on my observations, I'd bet she was either drunk or otherwise partially sedated. Maybe a date rape drug was used." She glanced at her notes on the desk in front of her. "I'll bet he picked her up in a nightclub. She was dressed for dancing."

"Louboutin pumps," said Meredeth.

"So dancing and a little woo-woo after the club closed."

"Woo-woo?" asked Cliff with a grin. "I hate it when you use medical terms."

"Shut up, McCloe," she said without looking at him. Her gaze kept straying to Van Zandt.

"I saw her *in situ*," said Meredeth, "but I didn't want to disturb the body and risk fouling some evidence. Any blows to the head?"

"Possibly," said Winchester. "I'll know when I cut."

"And when is that scheduled?"

"Tomorrow, first thing. I can call you with the results." Her gaze went to Bobby's, and he smiled.

"Sure. Here's my card," he said. "Call me any time, day or night."

"Thanks," said Nina. "I'll do that."

Meredeth glanced at Bobby and rolled her eyes.

CHAPTER 36

BREAKING UP IS HARD TO DO

David Branch's Farm, NY

CARL AND MICHELINA spent more and more time together, and their father had returned from Mack's final exam sans truck, sans Mack. They spoke about it a few times, wondering what it meant, wondering if Mack was out there, hauling freight back and forth across America already.

Both wanted off the farm as soon as they could arrange it. Michelina spoke of her ideas on where she would live (far away) and what she might do for a living (something involving computers). What she didn't know, however, is what Father expected of her.

Carl knew, though. He knew what was expected of him and what was expected of her. For his part, Carl was forming a plan for his life, and he thought California had a nice ring to it. Twenty-nine hundred miles away from the farm had a nice ring to it. Most of all, he was looking forward to getting away from the kids on the farm. He'd figured out how to please their father, but the kids—one girl in particular—left him frustrated and wondering.

"You could come with me," he said. "I'll be in school a while, and you'll need to get a degree as well. Maybe UCLA or Berkley."

"We'll never get into schools like that, Carl," said Michelina. "No high school transcripts, no standardized tests, no money."

"Maybe," he said a little defensively. "But maybe not. Father can get things done. He faked Mack's truck driving school and got him a license. He might do the same for us if he sees usefulness in what we want to do. We could live together, just you and me."

She smiled at him, one part bashful, one part excited. "You'd want to do that?"

He shrugged. "Why not?"

Michelina snuggled next to him and put her head on his shoulder. "That's sweet."

"Then you'll do it?"

"Let's see what we have to do before we decide where to go."

"Sure," he said.

That was when he noticed the dark form across their little clearing, that was when he noticed Lucy watching them. "Don't look," he whispered, "but Lucy's watching again."

"*Uffda*. That girl!"

"*Uff*-what?"

"Something my mother used to say. It's Norwegian or something. It means something like *oy vey*."

"Shh," he said. "We're not supposed to speak of the time before."

"Yeah, I know," she said.

"Or even admit to remembering it."

"Who said I did that?" she asked, then laughed. "You're not going to turn me in, are you?"

He watched the dark form detach from the trunk of the tree across the clearing, watched Lucy's shoulders slump as she turned away. "Why won't she let it go?" he murmured.

"Because you're awesome, Carl. Sex with you is amazing, and you're tall, dark, and handsome."

He chuckled. "All that?"

"And more," Michelina added in a solemn tone.

"Should I go talk to her? What do I say?"

"No, let me talk to her," said Michelina. "Girls can talk about things that a guy and a girl can't."

"Okay," he said with a shrug.

"Let me get dressed, and I'll—" Her words were lost in a soft shriek as Carl flipped her onto her back as though she weighed no more than a tissue.

"Not yet," he said as he rolled on top of her.

CHAPTER 37

LONG LIZ

Sherman Oaks, CA

DRUITT LOOKED DOWN at his Long Liz, and she looked back at him with dead, glassy eyes. He chuckled at the way fate sometimes told him he was on the right track. He'd spent an hour and a half looking for whores, then after he'd given up, a nurse from Kindred Haven was right there, turning the corner into the alley parking on the west of the hospital. It had been all too easy to pull in behind her and jam her into the trunk. No one had seen a thing, and as he drove away sedately, he'd wanted to shout his joy to the world.

He knew just the place to take her. The perfect place for a play date, where no one would interrupt, no one would interfere. Of course, he might have to call in an anonymous tip after he found his Kate, but he'd deal with that when the time came.

Then again, he was betting Connelly was smart enough to pick up the clues—especially if they found Kate before

Long Liz. She'd know she'd missed one by the snippets of Jack's masterpiece poem.

Hell, he might even give her a clue where to find Long Liz.

He drove a few blocks north, crossing over the L.A. River in its concrete prison, then pulled into the empty parking lot on his left. He drove around to the back of the building.

This was the worrisome part. Anyone on the Ventura Freeway would be able to see him drag Long Liz out of the car. *If* they bothered to look north. An alternative would be to go to the north side of the building, but with nothing by two cleared lots between the building and the businesses across Riverside Drive—or the residential area to the west—it seemed like the worse option of the two.

He pulled the car in front of the ramp to the defunct underground parking lot, then backed down the ramp, steering around the detritus of the remodeling project the abandoned building had enjoyed until the money ran out. He didn't want to do his business underground. He wanted to take Long Liz to the courtyard, to lay her out under the afternoon sunlight, then kill her, leave his poetry on a nearby wall and skedaddle.

After all, he still had to find a suitable candidate to play Kate, and it had to be today, now that he'd lucked into his first choice for Long Liz.

He backed the car into the shadows, then got out and got Long Liz out of the trunk. She was still out of it, so he threw her over his shoulder, grabbed his bag, slung it over the other shoulder, and then went to find the stairs up to the ground level. Old Liz weighed about one-thirty, he figured, using his calibrated shoulder to gauge her weight. He climbed the stairs with ease despite his burden, Long Liz's head bouncing off his shoulder blade.

He walked into the exact (or as exact as he could guess) center of the square courtyard and glanced up at the bright square of sunlight beating down on them. He bent at the waist and dropped Long Liz to the Spanish Mission Red tile square. He opened his bag and withdrew a woman's scarf, bent over her, and tied it around her neck—taking care not to tie it too tight. He pulled the fancy wooden case that contained his Liston knives out of the bag and set it gingerly on the tiles next to her head.

He'd have to be disciplined with Long Liz. He'd have to stop after the neck incision. Kill her, yes, but no mutilation beyond what was necessary. His inner demon didn't like that idea, not one bit, but he'd slake that thirst when he found good old Kate.

Long Liz groaned and turned her head to the side. She gagged but didn't foul the scene, which made him smile. He dropped onto her belly, his knees pinning her biceps to the red tiles, then he leaned forward and flipped open the case. She groaned again, louder this time, and flipped her head to the other side.

He didn't mind, though. He hefted the biggest Liston knife, then laid it across Long Liz's neck. That brought her around fast. Her eyes widened with surprise, and her mouth opened to speak, but he slashed across her neck as hard as he could, smiling down at her.

Long Liz began to struggle then, but it was already too late.

CHAPTER 38

CHEWING

Sherman Oaks, CA

THEY'D DECIDED TO call it an early afternoon after leaving the ME's office. They were in the hard part of a serial killer investigation—the place where waiting for the next body was the only real course of action.

Besides, Meredeth wanted to make a phone call or two.

She strode into her hotel room and closed the door behind her. Tossing her purse on the dresser and kicking off her shoes, she strode over to the little table and sat facing the window. For this conversation, she didn't want to see the bed. She didn't want to lose her nerve; she didn't want the temptation to smooth it over.

She hit Kevin's contact icon and put the phone to her ear. He answered on the second ring but sounded out of breath.

"Hey, beautiful. Have the superstar actresses banded together to drive you out of town so they can return to their roles as the sexiest women in L.A.?"

"You talked to Jim," she said in a neutral voice.

"Ah," Kevin said. "What did he do?"

"Well, I'll tell you, Saunders. He may have ruined Roger Shelton's career. He called the L.A. County Sheriff. He demanded they remove Roger from the investigation, and judging by how pissed off everyone was, he probably gave a tongue lashing about the inappropriateness of having a suspected serial killer on active duty."

Kevin was silent a moment, digesting what she'd said, no doubt, taking in her tone. "I didn't—"

"You didn't *think*? I'll say. I talk to you about my cases because I always assumed you kept what I said in confidence. Now, I'm less sure of that."

"Hold on, Meredeth. Let me explain. I didn't ask Jim to do anything. I just told him about Shelton and registered my concerns. I had to because I needed to ask him if I was playing the overprotective beau or if there was something real there to worry about. Evidently, he agreed about the last part."

"Dammit, Saunders, he *shouldn't have even known* about the situation. We hadn't reached a conclusion. We were still trying to clear him, *with his cooperation*! Now, I'm sure his cooperation is at an end."

"I'm sorry, Mere."

"I'm half-sure Cliff McCloe will be guarded and always checking what he wants to say, too. You've turned us into exactly what that buffoon, Jeremy Goode—may he rest in peace—loved to throw in my face. You've made his claim that I breeze into town and start making demands a reality. Now, I really am that person!"

"No, you're not, Meredeth, and everyone knows that. Listen, *I'll* call Detective McCloe and explain what happened. I'll—"

"Haven't you done enough?" she hissed.

Kevin said nothing for the space of a handful of breaths, then said, "Boy, I really screwed up, didn't I?"

"Yes!"

"I'm really sorry, Mere. I made Jim promise not to—"

"To drop it? You mean the same promise I extracted from *you*?"

"I apologize—"

"Say that one more time, Saunders, and I don't know what I'll do, but I imagine it won't be pleasant for either of us."

"Okay, I'll stop. After this: I feel horrible, Meredeth. I feel like I betrayed your trust—"

"Well, *duh!*"

"—and screwed everything up. I love you, FBI, from the top of my head to the soles of my feet. I don't know what to do to make it better, but losing you would be...would be...like losing Vanessa. Like losing my marriage of twenty-some-odd years. I don't want that to happen. Tell me how to fix it."

Meredeth closed her eyes and sighed noisily. "Why didn't you drop it, Kev?"

"Because of everything I just said. I love you. I don't want to—*can't*—lose you."

"I'm a field agent. You knew that going in."

"I did, and I—"

"You have to trust me to take care of myself, Kevin."

He fell silent, and she heard him sigh. "Yes, that's the hard part, isn't it?"

"Oh, I suppose," she said, her fury bleeding away into the radio waves between them. "And Bobby's always got my back. You know that."

"I do. He told me a year ago he's always your Personal Security Detail."

"Do you think he'd allow Roger to harm me? Do you believe he could be distracted from that security? Because I don't. To my mind, anyone trying to hurt me is going to face one pissed-off Force Recon Marine."

"But Alex got to you, and Bobby was there."

This time, it was Meredeth who fell silent. She closed her eyes and pictured Kevin's face, imagined his hand snaking around her waist as he liked to do, and she asked herself if she wanted to go back to living without all that. "Kev, listen to me. Alex was a fluke. We knew the Passe-a-Grille Killer was male. Sonya Sargent wasn't a male. She was a beautiful blonde supermodel type with a law enforcement job and friends who vouched for her. No one saw Alex coming."

"No, I suppose not."

"And Bobby did save me that day. If he hadn't been there, Alex would have finished the job."

Kevin took a deep breath and blew it out. "Yeah. You're right."

"What was that? There was a bit of interference with the call."

"No, there wasn't," Kevin said. "You just want me to repeat the fact that you are right, and I am wrong."

"There's that interference, again," she said with a laugh.

"You're right most of the time. You know that. Sometimes *I* am right, though, and all I wanted from Jim was for him to say whether I was right or wrong in this instance."

"And what did he tell you?"

"He said I was probably right."

"Then I guess I have to call him next and verbally kick his ass, too."

"Go easy on the guy. He lost his nephew recently."

"Yeah," she said, feeling suddenly exhausted. "Promise me, Kevin."

"That I won't do this again? Easy. I *will* never do this again."

"I need more than that, Kev. I need to know that *anything* and *everything* I say to you is between you and me—and *only* you and me."

"Done. I promise."

"And you won't go to our mutual acquaintances to find out that you're wrong."

"Mere, I don't ever want to have a conversation as scary as this one. Not ever."

"Scary?"

"Yeah, of course it terrified me. Didn't I just say how horrible losing you would be?"

"You did, but hearing it again isn't so bad."

"I need something from you, too, Mere."

"What?"

"I need your promise that you will take my worries seriously, even if you disagree."

"I suppose that's fair."

"Promise?"

"On Bobby's life."

Kevin laughed. "I suppose that will have to do. Are we good now, FBI?"

"I think we are, HRT."

"Yeah, I guess I can't go on calling you FBI when we're both in the Bureau. You called me HRT. Does that mean I can call you BAU?"

"Nah, nah. I like it when you call me FBI."

"It's settled then. Now, I have a very important question."

"Toilet paper is in the hall closet."

"Yeah, I found that. My question is more important than toilet paper."

"Okay, I'll bite. What's your question, HRT?"

"What are you wearing?"

Meredeth threw her head back and laughed long and hard.

CHAPTER 39

RED ROVER, RED ROVER, SEND KATE ON OVER

Sherman Oaks, CA

MICHAEL DRUITT DROVE in circles, great huge circles around Sherman Oaks. The truth of it was that he didn't know where to find his Kate. He'd thought he had a month before he needed Long Liz and Kate, but thanks to Connelly, he'd had to compress his forty-six-day plan into four, and that didn't sit quite right with him. But he supposed it was his own fault for choosing a place like Los Angeles. He'd thought the massive population would provide cover—like a haystack did for a needle—and with his other victims, it had. Of course, he'd wanted to honor Jack the Ripper, and evidently, the detectives in LASD weren't quite as stupid as he'd hoped.

He'd checked all the places where he used to find whores, and they were all *empty*. No hookers, no johns, no cops keeping watch. It was as if prostitution had been eliminated in Sherman Oaks and Van Nuys, but he knew that couldn't be true. He believed whores *needed* their work in the same way that heroin addicts needed their horse. But he must have fallen out of touch, and it wasn't as though he could call one of those tour companies and ask where the whores hung out.

He'd heard about other strolls in L.A., but the ones he knew still did a roaring business were in parts of town he didn't want to go. Yes, he was a serial killer, but that didn't mean he had carte blanche to go wherever he pleased. He still needed to worry about his personal safety, and though his fleet of "work" cars might fit in anywhere, his skin color wouldn't.

But he knew a place, if YouTube could be believed, and it was relatively close to his base of operations: West Hollywood. He jumped on US 101 and drove southeast through the Hollywood Hills. Fifteen minutes later he was driving west on Hollywood Boulevard, telling himself that if he didn't find Kate there, he'd cruise the Sunset Strip. Between the two, he believed he'd find someone suitable, if only by reputation.

In the end, he found her walking down Sunset, her glittery bag hanging from one limp hand, her tiny little dress riding up, her head tilted forward, shoulders slumped. But she was the right age—about the same as

Connelly give or take a few years—and in the same world-beaten state. He pulled up beside her and blipped the horn, then rolled down the window. "Hey, beautiful," he called.

She looked at him sidelong and laughed. "Is Kate Moss around and I missed her?"

"You're prettier than her," said Druitt, though he had no idea who Kate Moss actually was.

"Yeah, and I suppose you're the prince of Egypt."

"Egypt?" he asked.

"Never mind. I was on my way home, but since you made the effort... What are you looking for?"

"Someone warm, alive."

She threw back her head and laughed, and Druitt had to hide his pique—at least for a while more. "Low standards, huh?"

"No, not at all. I've been looking for you all day. Mind if I call you Kate?"

"Suit yourself, champ. You still haven't answered my question, though. What are you looking for?"

"Everything you've got, Kate."

"Around the world, huh? One-fifty."

"Sure," he said, though Druitt had no idea what "around the world" meant.

"Want to go to a hotel or do the business in the car?"

"I've got a spot."

"Close?" she asked, narrowing her eyes and peering into the car.

"Yeah, very. And you don't have to worry. That serial killer stays up in Sherman Oaks with the fancy people."

Again, Kate threw her head back and cackled at the black sky. "I like you. What's your name?"

"Call me Jack," he said.

She put her hand on her hip and showed him a smile that she probably thought would light his groin up like a bolt of lightning. Michael found it sordid and ugly. She was a slut, a whore. She had no business believing she could turn a man like him on.

"Well, okay, Jack. Let's get it on." She walked around to the passenger door of the car, opened it, and slid inside. She slid across the wide bench seat until her left side touched his right side. She put her hand on his thigh. "Let's get the party started. This bit is gratis, but I want to see what you've got to play with. She worked her small, dirty hand up his thigh and into his groin. "Mmm, tiger, you've got a real piledriver there. I might have to give you the whole night gratis."

Gingerly, he lifted her hand away from his groin. "You keep doing that, and chances are I'll crash this boat and kill us both."

"Then let's get a move on, Jack. Hurry, you've gone and made me hot."

"Sure," he said. He put the car in gear, expecting her to slide away a little, but instead, she put her head on his shoulder and sighed with contentment—but whether it was for real or just an act he had no idea. He dropped his left hand to the armrest on the door.

She never even saw the syringe coming.

CHAPTER 40

FINDING KATE

Sherman Oaks, CA

MEREDETH SHUDDERED AT the sound of her phone trilling in her ear like an incessant demon tasked with driving her insane. "Hold on a second, Kev," she said. She glanced at the caller ID and frowned. "It's Bobby. Give me a second."

"Fine by me, beautiful."

She grunted at that but smiled a secret smile. She swapped to the new call and said, "Van Zandt, if you're calling to ask for advice on how to treat Dr. Winchester, I've got nothing but a knuckle sandwich for you."

"Saddle up, partner," Van Zandt said. His voice was all business, solemn and hard.

"Why? What's going on?"

"Some kids looking for a place to make out found a body. Female, mid-forties. She's in rough shape, and the girl had to be sedated. She's in Kindred Haven, actually, for monitoring."

"Oh, Christ. Where?"

"Near Coldwater Canyon Park."

"As in Coldwater Canyon Avenue? Where we found the second victim this morning?"

"Yeah. Interesting coincidence, isn't it?"

"Give me a minute to tell Kevin goodbye."

"Meet me in the lobby in ten minutes."

"Roger that."

"Oh, and Mere?"

"Yes, Bobby?"

"Wear your scene boots. This one's ugly."

"Understood."

Bobby clicked off without another word, and Meredeth switched back to Kevin's call. "Gotta go, honey," she said.

"Another one? Already?"

"Affirmative. Bobby said it's rough."

"Christ."

"That's what I said. I'll tell you what we find later."

"Absolutely. Get going."

"Thanks for understanding."

"Hey, someone told me you're a field operative. It comes with the territory. But be careful."

"Will do, but I'm going to be in the middle of like six hundred cops."

"And if they let you get hurt, I'm bringing the HRT out there."

"Love you," she said.

"I love you, too."

She disconnected and then ran around the small room like a whirling dervish, looking for the scene-appropriate clothing she'd worn since that morning and discarded as she and Kevin made up long-distance. She pulled on her undergarments, then the BAU polo shirt in navy blue so dark it was almost black. She found her jeans under the nightstand and slipped into them, then a pair of thick hiking socks. Her boots were over by the door. As a last step, she pushed her hair into a ponytail and donned an FBI cap. She took a glance at herself in the mirror as she used some mouthwash and found that her cheeks were still rosy from the make-up part of the call. She couldn't help but grin at the way they'd carried on like a couple of teenagers.

But she had to admit it felt good to have the air cleared and the inciting incident behind them.

She grabbed her bag, holstered her Glock, and slid it into her belt at four o-clock, her twin mag pouches on the other hip, then stepped out into the hall and ran for the stairs. Her room was only on the third floor, and she had an abundance of energy.

The stairwell dumped her to one side of the frou-frou lobby, between the elevator and the main entrance. Bobby wasn't down yet, so she found the hotel's coffee machines and made two cups, then thought about it and made a cup for Cliff. By the time she'd finished, the elevator had deposited Bobby on the fancy marble flooring. She waved him over and handed him a cup of joe.

"Cliff here yet?" he asked.

She shrugged, in the middle of sipping her coffee, and glanced at the double glass doors. She swallowed and said, "Let's go find out." As they walked toward the doors, however, the Impala pulled into the portico.

She took the front seat again and handed Cliff his coffee.

"Thanks," he said.

"What do you know?" she asked.

"Not much. It looks like a pro, and from what Patrol Division reported, he did a number on her. The word 'butchery' was passed on to me."

Meredeth frowned. "That shouldn't be."

"Why?"

"Because the next victim should be Elizabeth Stride," said Bobby. "The theory is that Jack was interrupted back in 1888. He killed her, but he didn't have time for his other tricks."

"No mutilation," said Meredeth. "This victim shouldn't be butchered. She should barely be cut up at all."

"Well, he's accelerated beyond any precedent, so maybe he's done away with the whole Ripper angle," said Cliff.

"How long until we get there?" Bobby asked from the backseat.

"Fifteen minutes. Less if I run the lights."

"Run them," said Meredeth. "And the siren. Get us there, Cliff. Get us there now."

"Yes, ma'am," he said, handing her his coffee to hold. "Everyone belted up?" He flicked the switch on the police console, and blue lights lit up the night. He hit a button, and the siren started to shriek. Then he raced west on Riverside Drive and screeched through the intersection onto Coldwater Canyon Avenue. "Straight shot from here." He raced south as the avenue narrowed from four lanes to two with parking lanes on each side, then into two lanes with a middle turn lane, and finally into a two-lane road. The road ascended into the hills and more rugged terrain.

Cliff handled the serpentine road like a professional race car driver, and Meredeth was very happy she'd buckled up. Most of her concentration was focused on keeping hot coffee out of her lap and off her hands. Approaching the intersection of Coldwater Canyon and Mulholland Drive, Cliff braked hard, then swung into a parking lot on the left that was filled with official vehicles. He pulled to the side of the lot and killed the engine.

"Is this part of the park?" asked Bobby.

"No. Yes." Cliff shook his head. "I have no idea. This is just where they told me to go. I'm guessing it's the closest accessible place to the scene."

"Let's go find out," said Meredeth, handing him back his coffee.

They exited the vehicle and walked toward the buildings at the end of the lot. There was a concrete walking path bordered by trees on the left and an array of nursery buildings on the right. The path curled around into a circle in front of the last building before the trees of the park took over. There was a circular patch of grass in the middle, and roughly every single member of the LASD stood around the closer half of the circle, looking toward its center. A large rectangle on the other side of the circle was taped off but appeared to be empty.

The LASD deputies made a hole for them, and Meredeth stepped through, then stopped, staring at the decedent's mutilated form. "Butchery was definitely the right word," she said as she pulled on a pair of nitrile gloves. "ME here yet?"

"No," said a faceless deputy in the throng.

"Okay for me to take a look, Cliff?"

"Sure. I don't think there's anything that could disturb this scene."

She stepped forward, careful of where she put her feet, and started taking an inventory of the corpse as she approached it. The woman's dress had been shoved up to her chest. Like the second victim, she'd been eviscerated, with her two piles of intestines placed over her right shoulder and in the crook of her left arm. A long, vicious slash had opened her abdomen from her sternum to her pubis, and visible stab wounds marred the skin between her thighs and genitals. Her liver also bore a stab wound as did her pancreas. One kidney was missing, and the other lay in place, exposed to the night air, but pale, bloodless. "Angry, aren't you, Jack?" she muttered. "At little old me?" Like the other victims, her throat had been savagely cut from ear to ear, and blood had coated the ground beneath her. Even one of her eyelids had been lacerated, and her nostrils had been cut, exposing her sinuses, with the tip of the nose detached.

It was an ugly scene, one that indicated frustration and fury, and not all of it was directed at the victim but rather in proxy for someone else. Someone who'd hurt the unsub, probably. Her own frustration ratcheted up a notch. "What's in the rectangle?" she asked over her shoulder.

"Graffiti written in what looks like the victim's blood," said another faceless voice in the dark behind her.

She walked around the corpse and ducked under the yellow tape. The unsub had written:

> *Six little whores, glad to be alive.*
> *One sidles up to Jack, and then there are five.*
> *Four and whore rhyme aright,*
> *So do three and me,*
> *I'll set the town alight*
> *Ere there are two.*
> *But the last one...*
> *The last one's ripest for Jack's idea of fun.*
>
> *You're not up to snuff, Connelly.*
> *You'll never catch me.*
> *So disappointing—I thought you'd be more fun.*

Meredeth shook her head. Something didn't fit. This was only the third victim of seven promised in the first and second poems, yet the unsub was already talking about the last victim. It didn't make sense, but then again, neither did seven victims, as only five victims were accepted in the official record of Jack the Ripper's crimes. Of course, there were twelve others, five before, one amidst the canonical five, then seven more ranging from immediately following the 1888 string of five, all the way to 1891. She shook her head, then turned back, intending to go discuss the poetry with Van Zandt and McCloe, but then she saw the ME's investigators pushing through the crowd of deputies, Dr. Winchester bringing up the rear. She put her hand on Bobby's arm as she passed, then raised her solemn gaze to meet Meredeth's.

Meredeth nodded a greeting; well aware this long-distance hello took place over the cooling remains of a woman. She moved forward, and Nina motioned her crew forward at the same time.

"Is CSI finished with the body?" she asked—something Meredeth hadn't thought to ask.

"Yes. They are examining the rest of the complex at the moment."

"Good," said Nina as she stopped next to Meredeth and turned to watch the ME CSI team cataloging the state of the corpse. "Let's roll her when you're finished with the diagramming. I want to see if there are wounds to her back."

"I doubt there are back wounds," said Meredeth in a low voice.

"I do, too. Neither of the other victims show any. But it pays to be a little chary in this job."

"I bet. I hope this didn't ruin your plans for the evening." Nina's surreptitious glance at Bobby was momentary, but Meredeth caught it. "Or interrupt them," she added with a lilt to her voice.

"Well, that's the nature of the job."

"I didn't see you at the scene this morning."

Nina turned her head and gave Meredeth a sly smile. "I was already nearby," she said in a whisper.

"You could've just ridden with us," Meredeth said in kind.

"I could have," said Nina, nodding. "I know it doesn't matter to you, but I can't say the same for all these gentlemen who are even now checking out my ass."

Meredeth chuckled, but it ended quickly as Nina's investigators rolled the body. Underneath it lay a color photograph. She moved forward for a better look. "Let's get a photo of this in place."

Nina came to her side. "Yes. Joanna?"

A woman in an L.A. County Medical Examiner T-shirt nodded and bent to the black bag at her feet. She withdrew a slick professional DLR camera and attached a giant flash, and Meredeth turned away until she heard the click-click of the shutter stop.

"Take a look, Meredeth," said Nina.

She turned and glanced down at the photo displayed on the screen of the camera. It showed an intersection, and that's all it showed. "Do you recognize it?"

"No, but I live in Malibu."

Meredeth beckoned Cliff McCloe over and showed him the picture. "Recognize the intersection?"

He nodded. "Yeah. That's the corner of Riverside Drive and Hazeltine. Westfield Fashion Square mall is on the southeast corner."

"What does it mean?" Meredeth asked.

"That's your department, Meredeth," he said with a small smile. "Maybe he wants us to go shopping."

"Somehow I doubt it."

"Mass shooting?" murmured Nina.

Meredeth shook her head. "Mass shooters are a different breed from serial killers. The unsub likes to be up close, to see the light die in their eyes. Cliff, send half of these guys to canvas the area."

"Looking for what?"

"Any sign of our unsub."

"That seems worse than sending them to find a needle in a haystack. It's like sending them to find a needle that might be in any of four states filled with haystacks."

"Do you have a better idea?" Nina asked.

"Hold on a second," said Meredeth. Something was coming up from the depths of her mind like a killer whale racing toward the surface while hunting seals. "This isn't right." She waved her hand at the decedent. "He's skipped Long Liz."

Nina's eyebrows bunched. "You mean there's a method to this madness?"

"A definite method," said Meredeth with a grim nod. She leaned close to Nina and whispered, "The unsub is a Jack the Ripper devotee."

"Oh!" Nina smacked herself on the forehead. "I wondered why the state of the bodies seemed familiar! I wrote a paper on the crimes for a forensics class I took after I passed my boards."

Meredeth nodded. "This one is supposed to be Kate, also known as Catherine Eddowes."

"Then the first body found was Polly?"

"That's right. Mary Ann Nichols was her real name, and the first victim was Mary Ann—"

"Blocker," said Nina as she rubbed her eyes. "This morning's victim was Dark Annie."

"What about Emma? Martha Tabram?"

Meredeth shrugged and said, "Maybe she hasn't been found, or maybe he skipped the victims that couldn't be verified as Ripper victims."

"Huh," said Nina. "I'll never understand serial killers."

"What did you mean about skipping Long Liz?" asked Cliff.

"The order of the Ripper's victims: Polly, Dark Annie, Long Liz, *then* Kate. But the unsub has done Polly, Dark Annie, and Kate. Where's Long Liz?" Her gaze tracked to the photograph as a technician put it in a clear plastic evidence bag. "That's a hint in case we're too dense to see the issue."

"A hint." McCloe crossed one arm across his torso and cupped his opposing elbow, then raised his free hand to stroke his chin. "I think there's a construction or demolition site on the southwest corner. Right across from the mall."

"Grab ten of these deputies and— No, grab fifteen and have them meet us there." She turned to Nina. "I hope you didn't plan on sleeping much tonight. There's likely another victim."

"No, I didn't," she said with a return of her sly smile and a glance at Bobby.

"I'll call you, Nina, if we find anything. In the meantime, you might want to call in another ME CSI team and get them deployed to Sherman Oaks," said Cliff.

"Will do."

Meredeth took one last look at the victim, then ran for the car. "Get a move on, LASD, this victim might not be dead!"

CHAPTER 41

LUCY WAS A DANCER

David Branch's Farm, NY

CARL BOLTED OUT of the farmhouse, a huge grin on his face. He ran up to the machine shed, which, in light of Mack's truck's absence, had become a sort of hang-out spot for the kids. His excited footfalls hammered up the hill, and as he crested the hill, Michelina stepped out of the shed. Her gaze searched his smiling face.

"Your final?" she asked solemnly.

"Yes! Father says I'm ready."

"Oh," she said and half turned away.

"Don't worry, Michelina. Your time has to be soon, now that Alex is gone. Father won't keep you here like he did Alex."

"Sure, because I'm not useful like Alex is."

"That's not what I meant. He kept Alex because none of us knew what he was looking for, not until Mack got his exam. All you have to do is figure out your methods, come up with a plan. Then go to Father and tell him. He'll make suggestions, but he'll let you run the show."

"And you, Carl? What's your plan? What's your test?"

He shook his head. "Father said not to tell anyone." He leaned closer and rubbed her upper arm. "Besides, you already know my best plan."

Her gaze returned to his, and she smiled a little. "Is he doing the paperwork you need?"

Carl nodded. "He said that's the easy part."

"*You're leaving!*" wailed Lucy from the doorway of the shed.

"Yes, Lucy. I'm going out into the world. I'm making my own way."

The diminutive girl closed her tear-filled eyes, streaking her cheeks with her heartbreak. "But we never got back together, and we were *supposed* to, Carl."

"I don't think so, Lucy," he said quietly. "But as great as you look, you'll have no problem finding another boyfriend when you pass your exam."

"Oh, sure!" she cried, then turned and ran around the machine shed in the direction of the wooded shield belt of trees behind it.

"Well, that sucked," Carl murmured.

"Come on," said Michelina, her voice filled with forced joy. "Let's go celebrate!"

CHAPTER 42

THE BAIT

Sherman Oaks, CA

CLIFF NEEDED NO prompting to run both the lights and siren this time, and he handled the driving with the same aplomb as he had on the way out. They rocketed down Coldwater Canyon Avenue, slid to the left at Riverside Drive, then Cliff put the hammer down in earnest and took the inside lane. Meredeth reached over to the controls and blipped the siren as they approached each intersection. Behind him were multiple LASD cruisers and SUVs.

Just like a parade, Meredeth thought.

She knew they were flying—the evidence was just outside her window, after all—but it felt like they crawled through viscous goo that slowly piled up and up and up. Finally, the mall appeared to the left ahead, and she wanted to *whoop*.

"This corner," Cliff said, his face a mask of concentration. "Taking it hot."

Meredeth blipped the siren—a series of short, sharp shrieks—and then they were sliding around the corner, the nose still pointing in the right direction as Cliff danced on the razor's edge of traction, the Impala's engine screaming like a trapped banshee. Then she was thrown forward against the seatbelt as Cliff jammed on the brakes, slowing, slowing for the turn into the decrepit building's cracked and worn parking lot. He ignored the construction trailers and drove directly to the wide stairs that led to the building's main doors.

Bobby and Meredeth popped their doors before Cliff brought the car to a halt, and the second he did, Bobby catapulted himself free of the car. He held his gun close to his chest, pointed straight ahead, both hands vicing the pistol's grip. Meredeth jumped out to follow and drew her own Glock. "Right behind you, Van Zandt!" she called.

Bobby's grip was unusual, the Glock slightly canted toward his right, his left elbow rolled up to apply extra leverage on the gun's frame to control the recoil. She never hassled him about it, however, as she'd seen firsthand what he could do with the pistol.

Behind her, Cliff's door opened, and footfalls chased her up the steps. Bobby had already dashed through the missing doors and into the lobby. He was making his way around the big space, his head and torso swiveling from side to side as he cleared places of concealment. Meredeth caught him up and put her left hand on his shoulder, lifting her pistol to point it at the roof.

"Get with Cliff," Bobby said. "I can go to one-man CQB. I was trained for it. Tell him to support you. He was in the Army and is good in the role."

"Affirmative," said Meredeth. She peeled out of Bobby's path and turned to find Cliff across the large room, moving forward slowly. She raced across the room and told him to fall in behind her, then worked her way toward the inside wall of the room, clearing hiding spots as she went. "Wait for us, Van Zandt!" she called.

He had almost made it to the inside wall and was approaching an open hallway that led to the north. He performed a tactical peek around the corner, flashing his Maglite into the long darkness.

Where the room opened into a hall on his side, there were locked double doors on her side. LASD deputies began to pour into the lobby and take up positions for suppressing fire should the need arise. She glanced at a deputy with corporal's markings on his sleeve, pointed at the double doors, and called, "Locked! Assign a team to clear it. And make sure we have this building buttoned up." Then she led Cliff over to where Bobby crouched, stabbing her own Maglite into the black maw of the hall. "This one's ours, Bobby."

He nodded and moved around the corner in a tactical run, as quiet as a snake. Meredeth and Cliff held back a little as there was no way they could match his stealth. "We'll clear the closed doors. Bobby will leave them to us."

"Ten-four," whispered Cliff. I wish we had vests."

"Our unsub is a knife guy."

"*Roger* is an excellent hand with a gun."

"Noted," she said.

The hall led around to another long lobby that faced Riverside Drive, but all the windows were closed with that white plastic construction companies loved so much. About halfway across the length of the room, a set of fancy wooden doors stood open, and Bobby glanced inside, then beckoned them.

"She's back there," he said in a world-weary voice. "She's down."

Meredeth drew a deep breath and hissed it between her teeth while Cliff radioed his brother and sister deputies. "We're going in," she said and walked toward the doors.

"Let me clear it, first, Mere," said Bobby, moving into the darkness with that combination of stealth and speed that amazed her every time she saw it.

"We can go together," she said. But it was no use as Bobby didn't slow or even acknowledge her.

The short, ten-foot-wide hall led to a pair of glass doors overlooking what must have been a very nice courtyard at some point in the building's history. The victim lay in the center of a square of red Spanish tile, directly under the giant square hole in the roof.

Meredeth had lost track of Bobby but knew he'd be in the shadows, observing the room, moving, failing to communicate, but given the need for stealth, both she and he knew that last part was optional. Even so, she felt slightly naked like she'd left the house without underwear. Cliff was at her back, and though she had no doubt he would provide cover and assistance if she called, it just wasn't the same.

She moved forward in a crouch, her pistol held at high ready. The moonlight painted a square on the floor that had the anxious energy of a minefield. She knew she should stick to the shadows until they were clear, but she also knew that if the woman was still alive, every second counted. "Stay here, Cliff," she said and darted across that moonlit field of red, squatting at the victim's side.

The woman lay in a partially clotted lake of her own blood, but the only mark visible in the light of the moon was a dark slash near the bottom edge of the scarf tied around her throat. Just like the original Long Liz. She felt for a pulse at the woman's wrist and could find none. She grimaced and put two fingers over her carotid artery, with the same result. She gazed into the decedent's face and frowned.

The victim was Liz Pacer, Mary Ann Blocker's party pal. That made it two victims from Kindred Haven Hospital.

CHAPTER 43

THE LAST ONE

Sherman Oaks, CA

FROM HIS VANTAGE, Druitt watched the trio scuttle around in the dark, a wry grin dancing on his lips. He watched his next victim dart into the moonlight and half-wished he wasn't constrained by his tribute to old Jack. He could have ended her that very moment, clearing his path to greatness and infamy that would rival Jack the Ripper—no, that would *eclipse* Jack the Ripper.

He watched as Meredeth sank down and checked for a pulse and had to resist the urge to laugh. *Does she think I'm so sloppy? Soon, she'll know how wrong that assumption is—firsthand.*

McCloe stood in the darkness but was visible to Druitt's night vision goggles, doing nothing but watching—all he had done since Druitt had dropped the first of the bodies he meant to be found. He redirected his gaze to where he'd seen Van Zandt stop and assess the wide-open space filled with darkness except at the very center.

Van Zandt wasn't there. Druitt hadn't heard him move, and the distance separating them was less than twenty-five steps away. He scanned the area—admittedly with more anxiety than he liked—zipping the twin barrels of his goggles left and right, scanning the depths of every shadow, every doorway. The man had simply disappeared.

At first, the idea scared Druitt half to death. The man could move, and the way he held that pistol of his spoke to special forces training and extreme competence. In a head-to-head gunfight, the result wasn't a foregone conclusion in Druitt's favor, and he never took chances with gunfights.

He worked on controlling his breathing—keeping soft, silent—while he watched Meredeth recognize Liz Pacer, his lips curling up at the corners, and he tried to pretend Van Zandt didn't exist. McCloe shifted from foot to foot, and Druitt spared him a dismissive glance. The detective could drive, but his tactical sense wasn't very good at all. He would be easy to deal with when the time came. The time that never would come until he got a handle on Connelly's Pitbull.

To his left, a door opened softly, then closed with equal stealth. He looked toward the sound, and saw nothing, meaning Van Zandt had left the courtyard or turned invisible. Either way, the time had come.

Druitt leaped down from the top of the paint and joint-compound splattered scaffold, landing with more sound than he would have liked but staying in the crouch he'd landed in, freezing in place, watching his next victim and keeping an eye on McCloe, who'd merely glanced in his direction. He counted to twenty, then rushed toward Connelly, his pistol rising out to his right as he ran, pointing at McCloe. As he crossed the line from darkness into the silvery light of the moon, he tore his gaze from Connelly long enough to send a string of five rounds at McCloe's torso. The detective probably had on a vest, and there was no way a 9mm round would tear through that, but it would knock the man down, and it would hurt like hell—hopefully giving him time to get Connelly wrapped up.

He switched his attention to her, raising his left hand to support his right and covering Connelly with his souped-up Glock. She rolled to the side, her own Glock coming up, tracking him, *targeting* him. She'd won a number of shooting competitions that he knew about—and probably a slew of them that he didn't. He couldn't let her draw a bead on him, or he'd feel the hammer blows of rounds impacting the steel plate in the plate carrier he wore. "Don't!" he shouted, and he put a round close to her, showering her with red dust from the tile he shattered.

She rolled and came out of it prone, her pistol tracking him once more. *Good grief! Just once, I'd like a victim who could follow directions!* He sent another round in her direction, but his concentration shattered at the last moment due to the sounds of McCloe getting to his feet.

Druitt whirled and sent another five-round string into McCloe's chest, then ducked and rolled forward, twisting around at the last second to come up into a kneeling position with his sites covering Connelly. He squeezed off the last round of the magazine, then with blinding speed won by thousands and thousands of repetitions, he performed a flawless tactical reload with a fresh mag. Connelly took the opportunity to move, flinging herself toward the edge of the moonlight, and it amused Druitt to allow her to make it.

He darted around the side of the square of light, moving to intercept her on the other side. Too late, he spotted Van Zandt lying at the edge of the wall, his Glock centered on him as if connected by an invisible string.

Panic and a fresh rush of adrenaline flooded into his bloodstream, and he fancied he could see Van Zandt's trigger finger tightening. He threw his weight backward, then gave up on that and dove for cover to his right. Van Zandt's pistol barked, followed by a heavy strike and searing pain that blazed through Druitt's left thigh.

When he hit the ground, he scrambled away, slithering like a reptile across the garbage-strewn and broken-tile floor toward the exit he'd planned on driving Connelly through. He made it to the door without further gunplay and risked a glance over his shoulder. McCloe hustled Connelly toward the front of the building, and there was no sign of Van Zandt, which was fine with Druitt.

Maybe he'd been over-confident. Maybe he'd made a tactical mistake.

Either way, his dream of ending his series with Connelly was dead. At least for the moment.

CHAPTER 44

FINAL EXAM

David Branch's Farm, NY

FATHER PULLED HIS new twenty-year-old Bronco around the front of the farmhouse and sounded the horn. Carl smiled at Michelina and squeezed her hand. "See you soon."

"Right," she said from behind a forced smile. "Do good, Carl. Pass. Stay alive. I'll look for you when I get out of here."

"Los Angeles," he whispered in her ear, then gave her a kiss on the cheek. He glanced at the others who'd gathered in the kitchen to give him a send-off of sorts—including the boy called Jack. "See you all."

He turned and opened the door to the porch, then stepped out and closed the door behind him. He ran down the steps and over to the Bronco. He flung the passenger door open and slid into the raised vehicle without any need to jump. He pulled the door closed, then glanced at Father.

"Ready, Carl?" the man asked in his dead voice.

"I am."

"You've remembered your knife case?"

"Yes, it's in my pack."

"Sharp?"

"Yessir."

"Did you say goodbye to your brothers and sisters?"

"Yes, all but Lucy. She wouldn't come to her bedroom door."

"I'll look in on her when I return."

"Thank you."

Without another word, Father dragged the gear selector into drive and took his foot off the brake. "It will take us an hour or so to get to our destination, but should you pass, you will thank me. You'll be in a town close to the Pennsylvania border, and you can hire transportation there."

It felt like the longest thing the man had ever said to him, and he nodded.

"Do you have questions for me?"

"Will I see you again?"

Father glanced at him, his cold, dead eyes assessing, probing. "Perhaps, in time," he said. "I'd like to come to your graduation if it's possible."

"I'd like that," said Carl, feeling the lump in his throat swell.

"But let's not get the cart ahead of the horse, here. First, you must survive your exam."

"Yessir."

"You understand the threat doesn't just come from me?"

"Yes, the local police, the possibility that the household will have a defense firearm."

"You must move quickly but in silence as I taught you."

"Yessir."

Their conversation wound down at that point, and Carl leaned his head back. He wasn't tired, but he didn't want to continue talking about the upcoming test, so he closed his eyes and slowed his breathing as if asleep. The monotonous growl of the offroad tires in conjunction with the drone of the exhaust almost put him to sleep in earnest. Or maybe it had because he didn't remember the passage of time, only that his father's big hand had fallen on his shoulder and given him a little shake.

"We're here, Carl," the man said.

"Yessir." Carl opened his eyes and looked through the windshield. A rotten little trailer sat alone at the end of the two-lane track, and it very much reminded Carl of his previous life. "Where is she?"

"Inside, son. You're a big man, like me. You have to be stealthy in almost everything you do. People will be intimidated just because you're big. They will shy away. It will be harder for you to charm them into your grasp. This test addresses all those points. The woman will be awake though she works as a prostitute and is up to all hours. She won't like you walking in, and she sure as hell won't *let* you in. You'll have to think on your feet."

"I can do that."

"I hope so, Carl. For your sake." He reached into the back. "I almost forgot." He handed Carl a folder of papers—no doubt his forged school and test records. Then he handed Carl a wad of cash. "For your travel to the West Coast."

"Thank you, Father."

"You're welcome, Carl. Now, get out and get to work. Assuming your success inside, this is our goodbye. If it goes badly, don't expect me to help."

"No, sir," said Carl, his hand on the door handle.

"Are you sure you want to copycat a crime for your test?"

"What better way to gauge my abilities?"

"Get to it, then."

Without another word, Carl opened the Bronco's door, grabbed his pack, and slid out. He paused a moment to slide the paperwork into his bag, then trotted to the end of the gravel track, ignoring the woods to either side.

As he approached the trailer, one of the windows slid up. "I'm not buying anything!"

"No, Ma'am," Carl said, putting on his best smile but not pausing a second.

"Who's in that car back there? The four-wheel drive?"

"My father," Carl said.

"Why are you running up on my house?"

"I need your help."

She cackled at that. "The hell you do, son. What you need is to turn around and get back in that monstrosity with your daddy and get the hell out of here."

Carl made a show of glancing over his shoulder, trying to look scared. "I can't do that. He'll hit me."

"As big as you are? Whip his ass, son."

"He's even bigger," said Carl in a sort of whine. "And he's strong." He'd reached her little patch of weeds, and in three more long strides, he was running up the six steps to her little slice of weathered wood deck-heaven. It creaked beneath his weight.

"What do you want me to do about that?"

"Nothing, but will you please just play along? I'm supposed to beg you for money, but if he sees me try, he won't be as angry if I come out empty-handed."

"Want me to call the cops? They can take you away from a man like that."

"Last time someone did that, the cops didn't do anything, and he almost killed me when we got home. He knows everyone around here. He's friends with the police chief."

"No police here, kid," the woman said.

"The sheriff, I mean. And he knows the troop commander for the state police barracks." He stepped up to the door and rapped on it softly. "Please?"

"God, my afternoon stories are on, kid."

"I won't talk. I'll just stand inside the door a few minutes, then go back and tell him you were broke until your check arrives."

"Ain't that the truth... Give me a second. These old bones don't want to move as well as they used to."

He stood there, trying to look scared, anxious, fiddling with the strap of his pack, shuffling his feet. The door opened, and he forced a timid expression onto his face. "Thank you," he said.

"Yeah, yeah. Make it quick."

She took a step back, and Carl took a step into the foul-smelling trailer. He pulled the flimsy door closed behind him, and the fifty-something woman turned her back on him and walked toward the front room. She was far shorter than him, closer to Lucy's size. She had dark hair like Lucy,

He set his pack down and withdrew the knife case his father had given him as a pre-graduation present. He flipped open the wooden lid and looked down at the three gleaming knives with a feral grin. He took out the biggest one and followed her to the front. *Thirty-nine stab wounds*, he reminded himself. *Five to the left chest, two to the right chest, one dead center, five to the liver, two to the lower left abdomen, and six a tad higher.* "Thank you for helping me, Ms. Tabran."

"Are you nutso, kid? That ain't my—"

The first blow from the Liston knife cut off her wind as it penetrated her left lung. "That's okay, Martha. I don't care what your real name is." His next strike was to the right of her chest. She slid out of her recliner, one hand trying feebly to protect herself.

The Liston rose and fell, rose and fell, repeating thirty-five times before Carl straightened and calmly walked into the disgusting slut's kitchen to clean up.

CHAPTER 45

A FINE IDEA

Sherman Oaks, CA

IN THE IMPALA'S passenger seat, Meredeth pinched the bridge of her nose, then dove into her purse for her bottle of Excedrin. Bobby and Cliff had given chase to the unsub, but he'd parked a car in the underground lot, right close to the stairwell, and he had gone blasting out of the parking lot, around the far side of the building, taking off down Riverside Drive. A few deputies had rushed to their cars to give chase, but it was as before: no one saw anything.

She hadn't been injured in the attack—at least not beyond her pride—but she was shaken up. The whole incident had brought her stabbing to the front of her mind, and she couldn't banish it to the dark depths of her mind once more. What was worse, the jerk had worn a mask and a night vision rig, so she hadn't even gotten a look at him. The way he'd handled the pistol, she couldn't help but think of Roger Shelton, and judging by Cliff's face, neither could he.

Still, it could have been much, much worse. For instance, he might have killed Cliff. He seemed to be able to put his round wherever he wanted—the same voodoo Bobby enjoyed. And if he hadn't been so dedicated to using her as a Ripper victim... She shuddered. Kevin was right to worry.

Roger Shelton or Dr. Aaron Gull? She couldn't decide who was her prime suspect. The gun argued for Shelton, but there was something about Gull that was vaguely familiar, though she couldn't quite put her thumb on it. Plus, there was the undeniable link to Kindred Haven Hospital.

Nina Winchester came over and knelt beside the open door. "You okay?"

"Sure," said Meredeth just as if her heart wasn't trying to pound a hole in her sternum. "Or I will be."

Nina nodded once. "I am a doctor. I could give you a script for something to help calm—"

"Thanks, Nina, really, but I can't take anything like that."

Nina nodded. "Did he hurt you in any way? Shrapnel?"

Meredeth shook her head.

"Want to hear about Long Liz?"

"Might as well, it'll take the attack off my mind if nothing else. By the way, her name is Elizabeth Pacer."

"Good grief this guy is sick," said Nina. "Wasn't the original Long Liz named Elizabeth Stride?"

"Yes, that's it: Elizabeth Stride," said Meredeth. "Even the modern victim's last name seems to play along. She was also a good friend of Mary Ann Blocker."

Nina shook her head. "I hope you catch him soon."

"Me, too," said Meredeth.

"Well, Ms. Pacer had the same mark as—"

Meredeth shot upright and stared at the ME. "What mark?"

"Three almond shapes and a circle, but all one uninterrupted line."

Meredeth closed her eyes, her stomach sinking. "A Celtic Trinity Knot."

"You know it?"

"Unfortunately. Do you see Bobby anywhere?"

Nina stood and looked around. She raised her hand and waved. "Bobby!"

He came strolling over, a small smile at odds with the stress lines around his eyes. "Hello, Nina."

"Meredeth wants you."

He circled around the Impala and knelt in the same spot Nina had just vacated. "What's up, Mere? Change your mind about the bus?"

"No. I'm not hurt, Bobby. Did you know the victims have the mark?"

"What?" He glanced at Nina. "All of them?"

She nodded.

"How did we miss that, Mere?"

"The marks were small and placed between the big toe and the second. I think he used a needle and black ink to make the tattoos."

"He's part of it," Meredeth said in an enervated voice. "No wonder he came for me."

"He knew all about you even before we came to L.A."

"Yeah," she said with an exhausted sigh. "This series was probably supposed to be bait. Something he knew we'd have to investigate, but his plan was that we wouldn't come until he'd dropped Polly, Dark Annie, Long Liz, and Kate. He'd be miles ahead of us. He'd have all his victims and drop spots ironed out, and the LASD would be frustrated already. I wonder if he always meant to use me as his last victim, or if he just thought of that."

"Michelina told us they were all fed a steady diet of the Exploits of Meredeth Connelly, Superprofiler. She said it was almost a religion with some of Ankou's kids."

"And?"

"Well, I only mean that—"

"Wait a minute!" Meredeth cried, excitement causing a tremor in her voice. "*Michelina*!"

"Yes?"

"She knows the male children Ankou produced. She knows what they *look like*!"

"Sure, a decade and a half ago."

"Don't you think you could recognize your brothers, even if you had been separated for a decade?"

Bobby thought about that and nodded. "Worth a try."

"Yeah. Find a picture of Gull on the Kindred Haven website. I'll find Roger on the LASD site. I'll text both links to her."

"Got it." Bobby pulled out his phone and started his search while she was already swiping through the LASD website.

She found her link first. She texted it to Michelina, along with the following:

> *Do you recognize this man?*

She'd forgotten the time difference, but Michelina answered almost immediately with:

> *No. Though he does look a little like a boy about five or six years younger than me. Ankou dubbed him Jack. I only knew him for about six months before I got away from that madhouse.*

"She doesn't recognize Roger," she said. "But he might look like one of the other kids who arrived right before she left the farm for good. Do you have your link?"

"Texting it now."

As soon as the text was delivered, she copied the link and sent it to Michelina. As she was typing a single query, her phone buzzed in her hand.

> *THAT'S CARL!!*

Meredeth dropped her hand to her lap and took a deep breath. "It's Gull. Roger Shelton may be a partner in these crimes. Go get Cliff. We need to get over to Dr. Gull's house before he clears out of L.A. altogether."

CHAPTER 46

EVASION AND ESCAPE

Sherman Oaks, CA

CARL CURSED UNDER his breath as hot sticky blood ran from the wound in his thigh down his calf and into his shoe. The wound burned like the Devil himself had taken up residence there, and he knew he had to get the bleeding under control, or he would pass out, then bleed out. It would never clot on its own. He had Celox back at the garage, and frankly, he couldn't afford the time to stop and treat his wound, not with half the LASD out looking for him. He settled for clamping his hand on the side of his thigh and jamming his thumb into the wound. It hurt like the end of the world, but he just might survive long enough to bring that wonderful end to fruition.

He threaded his way through back streets, always going south or east or both. When he turned onto Whitsett from Valley Spring Lane, he sighed with relief.

He turned south once more, then east at Ventura, and five minutes later, he was pulling the car into his storage garage, feeling lightheaded and battling the edges of his vision as they tried to contract, to turn black.

Carl didn't mess around with the cars—chances were, he wouldn't need any of them for a while. His leg would take time to heal—time he didn't have unless he curtailed his activities. The biggest problem would be work—he'd have to come up with a strategy or a good story as to why his leg was injured. Perhaps he could tell everyone he'd taken a tumble and torn his ACL.

He came awake with a surge of adrenaline. His hand had fallen away from his leg, and he must have passed out or fallen asleep. The reality of his situation wasn't lost on him—he was bleeding to death and had to address that immediately, or he might not be able to.

He pushed the car door open, gasping with the effort of it, and swung his legs out, stifling the scream that exploded from his chest by biting the heel of his hand. He lunged to his good leg, putting barely any weight on the wounded left one. He lurched across the room, half-hopping, half-stumbling, and made it to the old metal desk he acquired somewhere along the line. He jerked the side drawer open and found a packet of Celox and a box of gauze. He needed to soak the wound with iodine but didn't see the bottle he'd put in the drawer.

With his heavy eyelids gaining weight with every passing second, he bit one corner of the Celox envelope and ripped the top away. He pulled his thumb out of the wound and dumped the entire packet into the wound on the anterior side of his thigh. He thought the wound had been a through-and-through but hadn't exactly had time to do a proper triage as he raced away from the scene. He covered the entry wound with a four-by-four of sterile gauze, then felt the back of his leg with his left hand.

He grunted in disgust—the ventral portion of his thigh was as dry as a bone in the desert, meaning there was no exit wound, and the damn bullet was still inside. He wasn't prepared to remove it himself—not as woozy as he was from lack of blood. He needed to button the wound up and drive home. He had instruments there, he had a shower to wash off and cleanse the wound, and he could sit on the floor of the white tiled shower, pour iodine into the wound as he knew he should, extract the bullet, then use more Celox to stem the new flow of blood, dress the wound properly, then lie in his giant bed and enjoy the sleep of the righteous.

He opened a drink that was ninety-percent sugar and seventy-five percent caffeine and chugged it. He needed the energy to make it home. He found a candy bar in the top drawer and ate that as well. Then, using a chair as a cane, he walked to another of his anonymized cars. He couldn't risk walking to the parking lot—plus, he had no confidence he could make it without starting up the blood fountain again.

He started the car and drove it out of his storage garage, through the maze of corridors, and out into the parking lot proper. He backed in next to his personal car to minimize the number of steps the transfer might take. He opened the door, swung his legs out, and forced himself to his feet, gasping at the pain. He hopped out of the way, slammed the door of the "work" car, and opened his daily driver up, falling into the driver's seat with another muted shout of pain. He got his legs in and pulled the door closed, then pressed the start button and backed out of the space.

He was glad he'd found a storage place close to home because if he had to drive more than ten or fifteen minutes, he thought he might pass out. He cruised up into the hills, taking Rhodes Avenue to the very top. He owned a house that required a driveway that climbed to the highest point in the mini-canyon wedge between two taller hills. He paused halfway up and stared at the Mazda parked in his driveway. He killed his lights and stared up at the house. A dark figure moved around from the side of the house and approached the front door, pausing to peer in his dining room window.

With numb hands, Carl jammed the gear selector into reverse and backed away, careful not to squeal the tires or rev the engine up. He swung around in the wide part of the road, then drove back down Rhodes.

For the first time since he'd discovered Lucy's betrayal, Carl didn't know what to do. Michelina had never joined him in Los Angeles, or if she'd tried, they'd never connected. He'd read about Lucy's arrest up in Ukiah, but even if he hadn't, he would've never called her for help. That would have been foolhardy.

Father wouldn't have helped even if he hadn't gotten himself captured to set off the chain of challenges that made up the bulk of his and Uncle Kenny's grand plan. Alex *may* have helped, if he was in a good mood, and if he thought the situation warranted help—not that they'd ever been very close to begin with—but none of that mattered since Alex was sitting in a maximum-security prison in Florida.

That left only one real friend. Only one person he'd consider family. He and Mack had spent time together over the years. He'd offered Mack a place to stay, to relax and unwind. He'd also done Mack many favors with his prescription pad in the form of Adderall and other stay-awake medicines.

As he approached Ventura, he fumbled through the center console for his phone, then, at the stop sign, he hit Mack's number from his contacts and pressed the phone to his ear. He checked for oncoming traffic and pulled out, heading for the Ventura Freeway on-ramp via Coldwater Canyon Avenue.

He was fully aware of the irony but wanted the fastest way out of town.

CHAPTER 47

MAKING UP IS NEVER EASY

Sherman Oaks, CA

CLIFF PULLED UP at the foot of Gull's magnificent, megalithic driveway and pointed up the hill at the dark shape near the house. "That's Roger's car." His voice was shaky.

"Pull us up there next to the Mazda," Meredeth said. "Let's see if we can find him. He may still be involved."

"Wait a minute! Your friend said she didn't recognize Roger."

"But she said he did remind her of a kid she hadn't known for long. A boy who was named Jack."

Cliff shook his head but lifted his foot and drove them to the top of the drive. As they got out of the car, Roger stepped out of the shadows near the house.

"I can explain," he said.

"What are you doing here?"

"Aaron Gull is the unsub. Something about him set off sirens in my head—that's why I was at Kindred Haven this morning. I wanted to know if he'd had reason to be at the hospital while the body was being dumped, but I couldn't confirm whether he'd been there after hours or not. I asked the nurses, but none of them would tell me where Gull lived, so I left. After Marcus pulled me from the case, I decided to dig into the good doctor's past, and guess what? Aaron Gull didn't exist before he entered UCLA as an undergraduate."

"We know Gull is the unsub," said Meredeth in a quiet voice that made them all strain to hear her. "What are you doing here now?"

"I needed something to prove Gull was the killer. I came over tonight to... I wanted to see if there was something that confirmed my suspicions. I wanted to find something that would shift your suspicions away from me and center them on Gull."

"Lucky for you, the man already did that," said Bobby. "He attacked Meredeth at the last scene."

Roger's gaze jumped from Bobby to Cliff, and he arched an eyebrow.

"It's true, Rog."

Shelton looked at Meredeth. "Are... Are you okay?"

"I am," she said. "And I owe you an apology. I didn't rat you out or request the department pull you from the case. What I did was discuss the case with my slightly overprotective boyfriend, and he spoke about it to my boss. You know the rest."

Roger gave her an assessing look and a slow nod.

"So did you find anything, Jack?" Bobby asked.

Smooth, thought Meredeth. *He did that perfectly.*

"Jack?" Shelton asked, looking more than a little confused. "It's Roger."

"Right, right. Sorry," said Bobby. "It's been a long day."

"But I did find something," he said. "Follow me."

They traipsed through Gull's dark lawn, then around the side of the house. Roger led them to a window with the treatments pulled back. Gull (or maybe his cleaning lady) had left the desk lamp burning. It had beautiful walnut built-ins upon which ten antique Liston knife sets were displayed, each with a soft LED light focused on it. On the walls hung several paintings—three of the Trinity Knot in multiple colors and even an abstract that wasn't very abstract at all. But the last painting grabbed Meredeth's attention and held it.

It was a springtime landscape of a farm. A farm Meredeth knew all too well.

It was David Branch's farm near Yoagoh, New York.

CHAPTER 48

BLACK HELICOPTERS

Mojave Desert, CA

THE BLADES OF the black FBI helo thundered above their heads. They all wore a headset so they could communicate, though no one seemed to have much to say. While they had waited for the helicopter to get fueled up and then deploy to Sherman Oaks, Meredeth and Bobby had told Roger all about Ankou and his mob of sociopathic children.

A thousand feet below them, I-95 stretched away to the northeast like a magical quick-silver ribbon bisecting the desert. Headlights danced through Meredeth's field of view—cars headed toward L.A.—and taillights lit the other lane. One of those sets of taillights belonged to the car registered to Aaron Gull, M.D., though she had to take that on faith. A FLIR operator sat up front with the pilot, his head ducked toward the radar's screen, which showed a nightmare image of cars traveling below them.

The FBI had agreed to perform the tails since the LASD would be out of their jurisdiction, and more than twenty FBI vehicles trailed behind Gull at various distances, rotating often so he didn't see any particular car too many times in his rearview mirror. He was smart, driving a few miles per hour under the speed limit in the left-hand lane, forcing the tails to pass him, race ahead, and rejoin the chase after he'd passed.

All that stood between them and pulling Gull over and executing a felony arrest in the desert sand was the traffic. Meredeth hoped for a break sooner rather than later. She really didn't want to try tracking the elusive killer through the streets of Las Vegas.

CHAPTER 49

ESCAPE ROUTE

Mojave Desert, CA

CARL DARTED HIS eyes back and forth between the road stretching away into the desert in front of him and his rear-facing mirrors. His guts churned, and his leg throbbed with each imperfection in the road's surface, no matter how small. But his instincts, maybe just his anxiety, wouldn't allow him to relax. Something felt wrong, off in ways he couldn't name.

He kept thinking he was being passed by the same cars over and over. He knew he wasn't in the best state of mind due to the wound, the pain, and the blood loss, but still, those cars nagged at him. In particular, he was sure he'd seen a silver Dodge Ram pass him, again and again. Sure, the Ram was pretty ubiquitous, but he thought he'd seen the *same* Ram, not just the same model and paint color. The problem was, he kept forgetting to make note of the license plate as it passed.

Fatigue was nibbling at his thinking. He'd been awake for a long time—forty-five hours. His residency had trained him to govern his thoughts and emotions as his exhaustion grew, but residency had been a decade in the past, and the curriculum hadn't included a seeping leg wound. He wished he'd gotten to his house before whoever had been there poking around. Treating the wound would have made all the difference, and chances were he'd have caught a little shut-eye as well. He'd considered stopping and finding a hotel, but he had no supplies, and simple over-the-counter stuff wouldn't do him much good.

Thinking of home made him recall his collection of Liston amputation knives that he was leaving farther and farther behind with each passing mile. He didn't mind leaving the other stuff behind—it could all be replaced—but the Liston sets and his paintings all created a pang in his chest.

"But it's better to leave them than to have them taken away while I sit in prison," he said aloud.

The road blurred before his eyes, and a car in the fast lane laid on the horn. Carl jerked the car to the right and opened his eyes wide, blinking fast to clear his vision. The slow lane solidified, and he glanced in his rearview mirror.

A silver Ram changed lanes to pass him, and this time he was determined to get the plate number. He slowed a little more, to five miles per hour under the limit, and the Dodge shot past him in the other lane. He glanced at the plate. "Two G-A-T one two three. Two G-A-T one two three." He repeated it aloud a few more times, hoping it would cement the number in his memory. He didn't think it wise to try and jot the number down in his phone, not with the sloppy way he was driving. He slowed another few miles per hour and peered into his rearview.

An old green van lurked behind him. An American brand, of course, and it was possible the van stayed behind him because it couldn't possibly pass him. Something about that bothered him, perhaps something he'd read online.

He shook his head, returned his attention to what was ahead of him, and discovered he was weaving within the lane. He slapped himself hard, sat up straight, and cranked the air conditioning down to sixty degrees, hoping the three actions would wake him up and help him stay that way. He had a few more hours to go, and the last thing he wanted was to fall asleep and leave the roadway out in the middle of the Mojave.

He turned on the sound system and cranked up some heavy metal until his ears threatened to bleed. The thundering drums and chugging guitars always gave him energy, and a good vocalist did even more for his state of mind.

Taking a glance out his window as a car raced past, he saw a shiny black Lincoln and thought he'd caught the driver looking at him. He watched the car until he could no longer see its taillights, then remembered he was supposed to be taking down license plate numbers.

His eyes were heavy, so heavy. All he wanted to do was close them for a moment, to rest them briefly, to alleviate the dryness, and clear the grit out of them. He knew those desires for the exhaustion lies they were, but it was hard to resist the urge. He wished he had some coffee.

His eyes drifted back to the rearview mirror, to the ugly green van stalking him from behind. He didn't know why it was an eye magnet. In other times, other locations, he'd have dismissed it as someone else's problem, but for some reason, his tired brain insisted that particular van was indeed *his* problem.

It didn't make sense. Not much made sense to Carl at that moment, however. Not the cars passing in the fast lane, not the van behind, not the blinking lights he kept catching in the sky to his left every now and then.

The fire in his left thigh continued to spread toward his hip and his knee, and he thought that was significant, though he couldn't say why. He thought he *should* know why, being a surgeon and all, but it eluded him. He should have the leg elevated, but he was too tall to do that even in the backseat of his car, and besides, who would do the driving if he moved back there?

His gaze returned to the green van, the back of his neck prickling as it did when he thought someone was staring at him. "What are you looking at?" he asked it. His eyelids were so, so heavy. His eyelids felt like sandpaper every time he blinked. He just needed a moment to rest them.

The sound of a car horn blasting behind him brought him out of a fugue just as his passenger-side tires hit the wake-up bumps on the side of the road, and he jerked the wheel to the left, overcorrected, then pushed the wheel back to the right until he tracked in the center of the lane.

The horn behind him... He glanced at the rearview mirror and saw the green van again, and the back of his neck prickled. Another car blew by him in the fast lane, startling him and drawing his attention away from the van. It was a black Lincoln Town Car.

"Was that other one a Town Car?" he wondered aloud. "Was that guy..."

His head wanted to roll back to the headrest, but he was far too tall for that to be comfortable. He looked in the rearview mirror, but this time he didn't look at the van but rather the backseat. The comfortable-looking backseat. "Mack, can you drive?" he slurred. "I need to lie down."

A white Dodge Ram pulled up next to him in the fast lane and tapped the horn a few times until Carl looked over. He couldn't see up into the vehicle, though, his own car was set too low to the ground. He tapped his horn in reply, and the Dodge pulled ahead.

Carl peered at the license plate, knowing it was important. He had to know if it was the same white Ram as before. He tried to read the license plate but couldn't focus his eyes on the numbers and letters. "How many times are you going to pass me?" he asked the taillights of the pickup.

He opened his window, hoping the cool, dry desert air would help him stay awake, hoping the wind buffeting him through the open window would shake him up, keep him awake.

"Lucy, take the wheel a while?" He glanced to the passenger seat, expecting her smiling face and finding nothing. "What the hell am I doing?" he wondered. "Lucy's in jail."

The wind generated by his car's passage through the desert night was too much, and he rolled up the window. He adjusted the fan on the air conditioner and turned off the stereo system, limiting the distractions. The road ahead was dark, too dark. He flipped on his brights and peered at the road.

There was something he was supposed to do, but he couldn't quite remember what it was. He checked the rearview, almost as if checking to see if the van knew. His green stalker was still lumbering along behind him, and Carl decided to shake things up. He accelerated, quickly putting space between him and the van.

The gunmetal gray Chevy 2500HD was back, approaching fast in the inside lane. Carl peered at the mirror but couldn't read the license plate. It occurred to him that if he couldn't remember the plate from before, there wasn't much use in looking.

"G-T... No, no. It's a California plate, right? It starts with a number. Three? Seven?" He shook his head. "Come back to that. What were the letters? G-T-A? Grand Theft Auto?

Cool game." He chuckled at his wit, then remembered his intent to check up on the van. He glanced down at the speedometer and discovered he'd come off the accelerator and was poking along again at grandma speeds. He checked the rearview mirror and found that the green van wasn't in sight. "Hey, where'd you go?"

He shook his head. "Why am I talking to a van?" He chuckled and decided to rest his eyes for a second or two. It would clear up the blurry vision, get rid of the dryness, the irritation. He drew a deep breath in through his nose and let his eyes close.

He awoke when the passenger wheels drifted into the scree along the edge of the road. He jerked the wheel to the left, but this time, he was too far off the shoulder, and the front of the car slid to the left while the rear went right. Adrenaline slammed into his veins, and his left leg lit up like a giant bonfire at the beach. He fought the wheel to the left even more and kicked the brake pedal with his right foot, exacerbating the skid. He panicked then, spinning the wheel back and forth, alternating between kicking the brakes and flooring the accelerator as the car completed its first full spin, all four tires not only off the pavement but out of the scree and into the desert sand as well.

Round and round he went, the landscape blurring, dust hurled skyward, destroyed desert foliage flying in every direction. He gave up on the steering wheel, lifting his hands from it altogether, and jammed both feet on the brake pedal, then shrieked at the bolt of agony that burned from mid-calf to his hip. He remembered his injury, then, remembered the bullet still in his tissues, remembered the blood. At first, the car spun faster, but the unrelenting pressure on the brakes shed speed with each rotation of the car as it skipped like a stone across the desert pan. He glanced in the rearview mirror, checking to see if the green van had followed him off the road, but, of course, he only saw the spinning landscape.

When the car finally slowed to a stop, Carl shoved the door open and tried to get out with the seat belt fastened. He released the belt and fell out into the sand and grit. His leg sang a lament of pain, and he felt the warm rush of blood down to his knee. He picked himself up, peering into the dark desert suspiciously.

"Can't stay here," he said. "I've got to get to... Got to get to..." He shook his head and looked back toward I-15. The blue Ford F350 had pulled to the shoulder next to the green van and—

The green van! He turned and stumbled back toward the car, then saw how stopping the spin had caused the tires to dig into the loose desert sand. He walked around it and stared down at the license plate, not really knowing why, but it seemed important.

"Hey, buddy! Are you alright?"

Carl whirled toward the voice and found an old man (maybe seventy, maybe seventy-five) in an old Dodgers cap walking toward him from the shoulder. It was the driver of the Ford pickup.

Carl turned and ran parallel to the interstate, crying out with each step of his left leg.

"Buddy! There's no cause for—"

"Tricks!" Carl shouted and kept running.

CHAPTER 50

AN END TO JACK

Mojave Desert, CA

WHEN THE FLIR operator shouted that the vehicle was out of control, Meredeth, Bobby, Cliff, and Roger all crowded toward that side of the helo, fighting for a glimpse of the car out the window.

"Get us down there!" Bobby shouted.

The pilot pushed the nose forward and pushed the collective toward the ground. He pressed the rudder pedals and turned the nose of the craft toward Carl's vehicle. He gave the jet engine fuel and accelerated.

They fell forward and down, buzzing over the westbound traffic lanes at six hundred feet, crossing the median at three hundred feet, and leaving the eastbound lanes behind at a mere one hundred and fifty feet of air. As the helicopter approached the vehicle, the FLIR operator pointed to the east. "He's running!" he shouted.

The pilot rotated the craft around its rotor shaft and fed the shrieking jet engine more fuel, then pitched the nose forward again, skimming over the desert at fifty feet, maybe less. Meredeth unclipped her seatbelt and jammed herself between the two front seats. "Don't let him out of your sight!"

"Aye-aye," said the pilot.

They raced past Carl's lurching run, and the pilot spun them around again, paying no heed to Meredeth's unsecured position. She fell sideways into the jump seat behind the FLIR operator's position and grabbed at the seatbelt.

The helicopter dropped, settling to the ground with a *thump*, and Bobby threw open the door and bolted out into the night. Meredeth rolled to her knees and propelled herself out of the helo. She tracked Bobby as he ran straight at Carl, who seemed taken aback by the sudden appearance of a helicopter dropping out of the sky in front of him.

At twenty paces away, Bobby drew his Glock and aimed it at Carl's head. Meredeth knew at that distance, he literally couldn't miss. She heard him say something, but the *whup-whup-whup* of the helicopter's blades and the distance hid whatever it was.

Carl, however, heard. He turned, wide-eyed, toward I-15 and tried to make a run for the road. A silver Dodge Ram skidded to a halt in the slow lane, red and blue lights flashing, siren wailing. Carl saw it and shouted something, then tried to spin to the east, but his left leg buckled, dropping him into the sand.

Bobby launched himself at the tall man, landing on his back and shoving the business end of the pistol into the back of Carl's skull. "Don't you move! Don't even twitch!"

Meredeth ran toward them, holstering her Glock and reaching for her cuffs. Up on the road, two agents piled out of the silver Ram and raced across the scree to provide support. When she reached Carl, his eyes were closed, and he appeared to be asleep, but as she applied the cuffs, she noticed his skin was the approximate temperature of the sun. She lifted her face toward the agents coming down from the road and yelled, "Roll medical! Get me a bus, now! I'll be damned if he's getting away again!"

CHAPTER 51

WHAT BROTHERS ARE FOR

Mojave Desert, CA

AS THE AMBULANCE crew moved Carl onto their gurney, a long string of eastbound traffic rolled by in the inside lane. Meredeth watched them for a while, amazed at how the drivers seemed incapable of watching the road instead of staring at the agents arrayed on the side of the road.

Once he was on the gurney, the bus's paramedic started a central line and began pushing IV fluids into Carl's veins.

"What's the story?" Cliff asked him.

"Sepsis, probably. He has a gunshot wound in his left leg. He tried to bandage the wound, but it looks like as his delirium came on, he sort of forgot he was shot and tried to do too much. He's lost a lot of blood."

"But he'll live?" asked Meredeth.

"That depends."

"On what?"

"On how fast we can get him to a trauma center. He'll need surgery in addition to critical care."

Meredeth pointed at the black FBI helicopter. "Take him to the helo."

The paramedic looked at it, then nodded.

Meredeth heard the rumble of a big diesel mill and looked to her left. A white Kenworth idled next to them, the driver standing up and craning his neck for a look. She waved him on his way irritably. "Go on, get moving," she said.

Carl pushed up onto his elbows and peered around, his eyes unfocused until he saw the big white truck. "*What are you looking at?*" he shouted, waving the big truck away. The paramedic gently pushed Carl back down, and the white Kenworth rumbled away.

Meredeth watched it go, filled with a sudden and unexpected case of the hinkies. Something seemed familiar about the truck driver. Something she couldn't place. She turned to Bobby. "Did that truck driver seem familiar?"

"I wasn't really paying attention," he said. "Sorry." He yawned and sat on the Dodge's bumper, put his hands on his knees, and closed his eyes.

Meredeth turned back and watched the truck until it was out of sight. She looked toward the helicopter. The paramedic and his EMT battled the desert sand and the wheels of the gurney, both of which seemed dedicated to tipping Carl out onto the sand again. "What is it?" she asked herself. She got out her phone, a feeling of dread locking hold of her guts, and dialed Kevin's number.

"Well, hey there, beautiful. Did you get him?"

"Yeah, but that's not important right now. Go to the office and wake up my desktop. Find the folder called 'Cold' and open it. Inside, find the folder named 'Mile Marker 33.'"

"I'm on it," he said. That was one benefit of loving a guy that got what she did for a living—he jumped when she asked him to in a certain way. His feet slapped against the hardwood as he ran down the hallway from their bedroom to the home office they shared.

"Desktop is waking up," he said. "I found the cold case folder, found the Mile Marker 33 folder. What do you need from it?"

"Find the file age progression of the sketch resulting from Michelina's description of Mack."

"You got a name for me, FBI?"

"Something with Julie Fuchs and AgeProg in it."

"Got it. Now what?"

"Send it to my FBI email."

"Affirmative. It's sending. What's up, Mere?"

Her phone beeped and buzzed as it received the email. "Can't talk now, Kev. Gotta go."

"Okay. Call me when you can."

"Will do." She disconnected and swiped open the Bureau's email app. She found the email from Kevin and opened it, then downloaded and opened the image file. "Holy shit!" she muttered. "Bobby, wake up! Keys! I need keys to this Dodge!" she shouted.

Bobby was on his feet in an instant, clear-eyed and ready for action. "What is it?"

"That bastard in the white Kenworth was Mack! You drive!" She turned her attention to the agents standing around on the shoulder. "Give me the keys to this truck or so help me I'll shoot one of you."

The agents responded with laughter, but one of them tossed the keys to her, and she passed them to Van Zandt, ran around to the passenger side, and climbed up into the truck. Bobby slammed the driver's door about the same time she closed the passenger side. "Get after him, Van Zandt!" She pulled her seat belt tight and secured it. She started the spinning red and blues and blipped the fire engine siren multiple times as Bobby got the truck started and in gear. He punched the accelerator and wedged the Dodge through the line of slow-moving traffic and into the median, clicking on the four-wheel drive as he did so.

The truck's engine wound up and up as Bobby twitched the wheel to the right and left, avoiding things only he could see. Once they were past the glut of emergency vehicles and the tow truck for Carl's car, Meredeth blipped the Big Red siren again, and Bobby sent the truck careening back onto the roadway. Vehicles moved to the right, getting out of the way of the speeding truck in the fast lane.

They made it all the way to Barstow, faster than would have been possible for the big rig, but there was no sign of the Kenworth or of Mack. Frustration burned in her veins as Meredeth put out a BOLO for the truck, then emailed the image out to the local FBI offices for distribution. "I really hate those two men," she muttered.

"We'll get him, Mere. He can't hide forever."

"He's doing a pretty good job of it." She laid her head against the passenger window. "Get us back to L.A. I want a shower, a good night's sleep, and then I want to get out of here."

"Yes, boss."

CHAPTER 52

THERE'S NO PLACE LIKE HOME

Tacketts Mill, VA

EXHAUSTION STILL DOGGED her every step as Meredeth trudged up her front walk, dragging her bags behind her. She kept telling herself she should enjoy the win, but the unrelenting pressure of Ankou's master plan weighed on her mind—especially the magical way his puppets could disappear at will.

I don't know how you did it, and I don't know where you went, Mack, but let me tell you something: I'm going to make it my first priority to lock your murderous ass away from daylight. You'd better prepare yourself because I'm coming for you.

The front door opened a crack. "You going to stand out there all afternoon putting all the other women in Virginia to shame?"

Kevin, she thought with a smile rising from the depths of her mind and blossoming on her face. She let go of her bags and sprinted the rest of the way up the walk, shouldering the door open and charging into Kevin's embrace. She nuzzled his neck and murmured, "I have missed you, lover."

"Um, yeah, I missed you, too," he said, sounding uncomfortable.

It was then that she realized he was naked and standing in front of the open door. Laughing, she kicked the door closed and started pulling off her own clothes, Mack, Carl, and all the rest of them forgotten.

I HOPE YOU'VE enjoyed *Rhythm of the Knife* and are dying to read the next case. The series continues with *No Body No Crime*, and you can find it on Amazon: https://ehv4.us/4nobodynocrime.

To be among the first to know what I'm up to and when the newest book I write goes live, please subscribe to my newsletter at https://ehv4.us/vvjoinehv or join my online community at https://ehv4.us/discord. You can also support me on Patreon at https://ehv4.us/patreon.

You can find my complete thriller bibliography at https://ehv4.us/booksehv. I also write supernatural fiction, and you can find my bibliography under the name Erik Henry Vick at https://ehv4.us/books.

Books these days succeed or fail based on the strength of their reviews. I hope you will consider leaving a review—as an independent author, I could use your help. It's easy (I promise). You can leave your review by clicking on this link: https://ehv4.us/2revrotk.

AUTHOR'S NOTE

WE'VE GOT TO stop meeting like this, my friend. Wait, what am I saying? Let's meet like this a lot more often! I hope you enjoyed Meredeth's adventure through the crimes of Jack the Ripper. To get things right, I relied on research completed by my assistant, Ryan W. Fox. Any errors are either intentional or mine, not his.

I've always had an interest in the Ripper crimes. For one thing, it's the earliest known serial killer case (at least as far as I'm aware) but the similarities to modern cases are abundant. Add to that the unsolved nature of the cases, the close match between the original profiles of Jack and the modern profile generated in 1988 (one hundred years after the canonical crimes) by John Douglass and Roy Hazelwood (both of the FBI's BAU), and the plethora of suspects, none of which can be interviewed or investigated beyond monotonous searches through Victorian records, and it's almost the perfect mystery. We can look into it until the cows come home, but no one will ever know if the results are correct.

Serial killers rely on their ability to fit in, and Jack definitely had that ability. All we really know is that he was probably middle-aged and a resident of Whitechapel; he was probably seen as odd, but not enough to raise suspicion. I can't help but compare these probabilities to modern cases—especially the charm of Ted Bundy, the extreme hatred for women displayed by Richard Speck, and the brutality and charm displayed by Ed Kemper.

In *No Body, No Crime*, the story will also be based on an actual case—that of Richard Kuklinski, A.K.A. The Iceman Killer. In case you didn't see the similarities, *Sticks And Bones* was also inspired by real events (and suitably modified to work within my overall plot line for the series)—the case of Winston-Salem's Pazuzu Algarad. The disgusting nature of the house described in the novel was written with pictures of Algarad's actual home (which was condemned and destroyed following his arrest). Most of these plots come from my imagination, but you never know when I might slide in some cold, hard facts to spice things up.

Enough about all that. Did you know that I have a rotating Ask Me Anything piece in my newsletter? I do, and you can be part of it. Please send me your questions by visiting my Ask Me Anything Google form. If that form is down for any reason, you can also send me an email directly at berserkerik@ehvick.com. Please add the subject line: "Ask Me Anything Question" to help me stay organized. Of course, submitting a question means you need to be signed up for my newsletter to see my answers, and I'd invite you to join up by visiting: https://ehvick.com/join.

Also, please join my online community Discord server at https://evhick.com/discord. It's totally free, and after the initial overwhelm dies off, it's pretty easy to use. I hope to see you soon!

PATRON RECOGNITION

A B I G V I K I N G hug to all my patrons!

Special thanks to Dawn Bogue and an anonymous patron for being the first of hopefully many patrons of the upper tiers.

ABOUT THE AUTHOR

E.H. VICK is the pen name for critically acclaimed best-selling and award-winning horror author Erik Henry Vick. He specializes in pulse-pounding stories filled with nail biting tension—usually involving serial killers as villains and psychologically-flawed protagonists. As an author disabled by autoimmune diseases (also known as his Personal Monster™), Vick writes to hang on to the few remaining shreds of his sanity. He lives with his wife, Supergirl; their son; a Rottweiler named after a god of thunder; and two extremely psychotic cats. He fights his Personal Monster™ daily with humor, pain medicine, and funny T-shirts.

With a B.A. in Psychology, an M.S.C.S., and a Ph.D. in Artificial Intelligence, Vick has worked as a criminal investigator for a state agency, a college professor, a C.T.O. for an international software company, and a video game developer.

He'd love to hear from you on social media:

Website: https://ehvick.com
Facebook: https://fb.me/ehvick
Amazon author pages:
  USA: https://ehv4.us/amaehv
Goodreads Author Page: https://ehv4.us/grehv
BookBub Author Profile: http://ehv4.us/bbehv

11/7/23 — 11/11/23

Made in the USA
Monee, IL
03 November 2023

45744714R00195